SIU YOKE

SIU YOKE

TONG

PARTRIDGE
A Penguin Random House Company

To order additional copies of this book, contact
Toll Free 800 101 2657 (Singapore)
Toll Free 1 800 81 7340 (Malaysia)
orders.singapore@partridgepublishing.com

www.partridgepublishing.com/singapore

Contents

Chapter 1   Father and the War 1

Chapter 2   Matchmaking 11

Chapter 3   The Gifts 17

Chapter 4   The Disappointment 25

Chapter 5   Father Dies 31

Chapter 6   From a Cat to a Lioness 41

Chapter 7   Mother Returns Home 48

Chapter 8   The Fight 54

Chapter 9   The Preparation 58

Chapter 10   The Meeting 66

Chapter 11   Indecision Is a Nightmare 73

Chapter 12   Getting to Know You Better 77

Chapter 13   Violet's Suspicion 83

Chapter 14   Violet Meets The Yongs 86

Chapter 15   Unconscious Decision 93

Chapter 16   Is It So Difficult To Decide 96

Chapter 17   Meeting Yun And Maria 100

Chapter 18   Confusion and Confession 108

Chapter 19   The Decision 113

Chapter 20   The Final Decision 117

Chapter 21   To Do or Not To Do 122

Chapter 22   The Telephone Call 128

Chapter 23   No Turning Back 130

Chapter 24   The Final Goodbye 133

CHAPTER 1

Father and the War

The first bomb landed on Singapore soil, shattering everything around for over fifty metres. It was early morning of 8 December 1941, around 4.30 a.m. Japan had declared war. Their war planes had flown in from Indochina, where they had been stationed. Suddenly, for the first time, the people realised that war had actually broken out. For the past few months, there had been talk about it, and some had shrugged it off as just rumours. Now reality had set in. Chaos. The Japanese bombers' targets were actually the British military and shipping facilities further south of the island, but some of the bombs went astray, and a couple landed not too far from father's photography shop. The shop was located on the second floor of a corner shop house at the junction of North Bridge Road and Upper Cross Street. Much of his photography equipment was damaged beyond repair, but Father had no time to survey the damage.

That bomb changed everything Father had planned for the family and especially for Siu Yoke. He was going to save enough money from the business so that she could go on to study to be a medical doctor. Perhaps it was fate.

Everyone was in a state of chaotic panic. The siren had already sounded an hour earlier, but nobody had paid much attention to it. Everybody had been sleeping, and the siren had been sounded before on practice runs. Now the blasts of those bombs jolted them up.

"Wake up. Wake up," Father shouted as he rounded up Mother and Siu Yoke.

They ran out to the streets but did not know which direction to go. All of their sleepiness disappeared, instantaneously replaced by fear and anxiety. Fire and the smell of smoke enveloped them as they reached the road, which was now scattered with debris of all sorts. Familiar buildings were unrecognizable except by where they used to stand.

Power lines and streetlights were down, but the roads were illuminated by the fires that were burning everywhere. Through the thick smoke, they could see people running frantically like headless chickens, shouting and crying. Some parents searched for lost children. The thick smell of burning rubber choked them as Father tried to find a way to safety.

Soldiers and policemen were everywhere, giving directions and instructions. People were shouting, crying, and cursing all at the same time, some screaming at the British soldiers, blaming them for not being alert and having allowed the invaders to get this far.

In the meantime, Father, Mother, and Siu Yoke were rounded up by some British soldiers and herded into a huge hall in one of the abandoned buildings along Upper Cross Street. The hall had been used as a meeting place by some clan members, and it was big enough to shelter a large number of people. Still they were all packed in there like sardines in a can. The hall gradually got stuffy and smelled of perspiration. Children cried continuously while mothers tried to calm them. When the raiders-pass signal was sounded, everybody stepped out of the hall cautiously and with much trepidation.

That was just the beginning. The Japanese continued their frequent air raids, day and night, until the British surrendered in January 1942. It was devastating, with people losing homes, possessions, and most of all, families. There were bodies lying all over the roads and under the rubble, and the soldiers and workers scurried to pick them up as quickly as possible to prevent diseases spreading from the rotting corpses.

Father and mother, with Mother carrying Siu Yoke in her arms, walked back to what used to be their home, which was now wrecked beyond recognition. They stood on the road, staring helplessly at the wreckage, recognising some of what had been the display cabinets that had stood proudly at the doorway to Father's shop. Now they were useless pieces of wood and scraps. The light stands were tangled in a web of twisted mess, piled up with the rest of the other debris, all strewn together as if somebody had just trampled on them in a show of rage and fury.

Father stood there feeling lost. Siu Yoke held on to Mother's hand, sniffling away a hidden sob.

"Mama," she cried, "I'm hungry." That was all she could think of then in her innocence although she was frightened and did not understand what war was like. She just knew that something bad had happened.

Mother looked down at her with tears welling in her eyes; and then she bent down to pick her up, to comfort her and assure her that everything was going to be all right.

"Don't worry, dear," Mother said. "We'll go to Grandpa's home. There we'll get you something to eat."

Mother turned to Father, who was still standing there looking at the ruins.

"Loh Kong," she said, using the Cantonese word for *husband*, "no use standing here like this. Let's go to Father's home."

Grandfather's house was about a twenty-minute walk away. There would be some food there, if the house was still standing. They also needed a place to stay, since their home had been destroyed. Grandpa's house was big with enough rooms to spare.

Without saying a word, Father proceeded to walk, obviously devastated by what had happened.

Siu Yoke was nine years old when the war came in December 1941.

* * *

I have no recollection of Father at all. He died at the relatively young age of forty-four when I was a mere two years old. I've been told he had tuberculosis. What little I know of him was from Siu Yoke. She had great admiration for him; he was her hero. He doted on her, as she was his precious jewel and his angel. Mother didn't talk much about him. In fact, she never spoke of him at all during all those years that she was alive. It was an Asian thing not to talk to children about their parents' affairs, I suppose.

I called Siu Yoke *Ka Xie*, which means *elder sister* in Cantonese. She had said that Father was a pretty quiet person, always keeping to himself, albeit a talented musician who played the erhu – a two-stringed Chinese instrument – for a Chinese orchestra in the club he was a member of. He was also a very good photographer.

His photography shop on that second floor at the corner of Upper Cross Street and South Bridge Road was his other pride, until it was damaged by that bomb explosion. He was devastated when that happened. At that time in the 1940s in Singapore, his skills as a photographer were ahead of his time, and he was well known throughout our small island country. His was the only photography shop in Chinatown at that time. For backdrops he used huge canvas paintings of countrysides depicting trees, rivers, houses, beaches, and so on. He had a skylight in the ceiling that was concealed by a sliding panel. By pulling a strong rope, he could open or shut it whenever he needed to allow the sunlight to come through or not during the day. That way he saved on electricity.

Siu Yoke was his favourite model, and he took many photographs of her in various poses and proudly displayed many of them in the display cabinets as samples of his fine work.

A movie director from Hong Kong came by one day. He had been looking at her photographs in the display cabinets. He was a distinguished, fine-looking middle-aged Chinese man sporting a slim moustache, a grey jacket, and black pants – like a European outfit – when he first appeared at Father's shop one day. He wanted Ka Xie to work for him as a child actor in Hong Kong. In her youthful beauty he saw the potential for the Hong Kong movie industry. There was room to develop her into a child star, he said. However, Father could not agree to that. He could not let her go to such a faraway place all by herself, and he was not prepared to leave Singapore.

"My daughter is too young to be leaving her family behind," Father said.

"But I will reward her and you handsomely. With her beauty, it is only natural for her to become famous and popular," the director said.

"I'm sorry, but my decision is final," Father said.

With that the director left – but not without these final parting words: "I really do hope you will reconsider my offer. She can be a great star one day if given the opportunity. I will see to that."

Father said nothing and bade him good-bye.

Nothing further was heard from the director. Some years later, another child in Hong Kong was discovered, and she was groomed for the movies and became very popular and famous around the Asian Chinese community. This child actress, Fong Po Po, later became equally famous as she grew up to be an adult actress.

When the war came, and having heard so much about atrocities that had been committed by the Japanese, Father instructed Siu Yoke to have her hair shaved and to dress as a boy. The Japanese soldiers had been known to take advantage of girls, irrespective of how old they were.

The invaders were merciless, and they made sure the people knew that. They systematically rounded up Chinese people, young men especially, who were perceived to be hostile elements against the Japanese. The invaders loaded the prisoners onto trucks to unknown destinations, never to be heard nor seen again. It was frightening every time there were knocks on doors in the middle of the night, and cries broke the still of the night when people were dragged out of their homes in the neighbourhood. Father and Mother had by now settled in at Grandfather's house.

The Japanese soldiers had instilled fear into everyone by being extremely unreasonable.

Father and Mother would hide Siu Yoke under a false bottom of the floor at the back of the house each time they heard the soldiers coming by, despite having already disguised her as a boy.

On one of these nights when they heard the trucks rolling by, mother quickly carried Siu Yoke to the small opening on the floor and lowered her into it, telling her to keep as quiet as possible. They had a pillow and a blanket in there to keep her comfortable, but the odour of the confined space made her want to vomit. She knew she had to control herself and be grateful for the safety.

"Keep as quiet as you can, dear," Mother whispered to her as she placed a table over the hole. The space was just big enough for a small body like hers.

Almost immediately, there was a banging on the door. The Japanese soldiers were not polite. They didn't knock on people's doors; they banged on them with their rifle butts.

"Open. Open up!" they shouted in Japanese.

Father rushed to open the door, only to be pushed aside by the invaders as they stormed in. Mother cowered in a corner, fearing for her safety. She had made herself look much older and untidy. She kept her hair unkempt to distract the Japanese soldiers noticing her.

The soldiers came trudging in unceremoniously, ripping open cupboards and everything else they felt could hide a person. Their stench of perspiration from the months of marching and combat suffocated Father and Mother as they searched the house. They turned the bed upside down, searching and poking their bayonets into everything, ripping the mattress and pillows.

Under the floor boards Siu Yoke was perspiring with fear and anxiety. She did not know what was happening but knew that these were not nice people. Through tiny cracks in the floor she could see the soldiers hovering above, shouting and gesturing in their Japanese language that nobody understood. Suddenly they stopped moving and stood only a few feet from where she was hiding as though they sensed something there. Fear gripped Father, Mother, and Siu Yoke. She closed her eyes and held her breath. For a moment the Japanese soldiers were quiet. Then they heard a shout from outside the house. Their leader appeared at the open door and shouted something, and the two soldiers made a hurried exit, following their leader.

"*Hai hai*," they responded to their leader as they ran out of the house.

Outside there was shouting and more screaming as Father shut the door in relief. The soldiers had found who they were looking for – an "undesirable" man who had been hostile towards them. They dragged him away, leaving his family and loved ones crying and screaming behind them. The truck rolled away with their captive, but the cries of the neighbouring family could not be silenced.

Father did not let Siu Yoke out from her hiding place yet. It was still too risky. They had to wait a while longer, until everything was really quiet. Until then Siu Yoke had to wait patiently under the floor boards. Most times, she fell asleep while waiting, tired in the dark, musky-smelling hole.

Events remained quite tame after the Japanese had rounded up all they wanted to, leaving only the passive, harmless citizens behind. At least 25,000 to 30,000 young men went missing during that time, although the official figure given by the Japanese was 5,000. A Japanese newspaper correspondent, Lt. Col. Hishakari Takafumi, claimed that the plan was to kill at least 50,000 Chinese, and half that number had been reached when the order was received to cease the operation.

This was the infamous Sook Ching operation, and it succeeded in instilling fear among the Chinese population. After the war, though, this fear turned into anger and then hatred. In later years, several of the Japanese officers were charged with war crimes and tried in Singapore. All seven officers were found guilty. Five were given life sentences, while two officers, Lt. Gen. Saburo Kawamura and Lt. Col. Masayuki Oishi, were sentenced to death.

In the meantime, Father's father had, with three of Father's brothers, fled the country for Hong Kong. He told Father to stay behind and wait for his return, when he would come back for Father and the rest of their family. He didn't make it. He died not long after establishing another family in Hong Kong.

Father was very disappointed, but he knew he had to continue taking care of his own family in Singapore and move on. Life was not easy after the war though. He didn't have enough money to restart his photography business. Many local businesses had been badly affected by the war, and many business owners found it difficult to pick up the pieces. Father was one of them. He started working odd jobs to make ends meet. There were not enough jobs to go round at that time.

The family had to stay with relatives from Father's side, and sometimes from Mother's side.

Mother's parents were well-to-do. Their restaurant business had not been affected by the war much. People had to eat. After the war, my maternal grandparents, in fact, increased their business by expanding their restaurant to two floors. Previously, they'd only had the ground floor for their business.

So Mother worked at her parents' restaurant, taking orders, collecting money, and generally helping out wherever she was needed. This helped the family income, and Father was grateful for that, although he didn't want to get involved in that restaurant business.

Unfortunately, good fortune didn't last long with her parents' business. Her father had been gambling. In one of his gambling bets, he lost his shop and his row of houses along Club Street. That was the end of her parents' little empire. They were reduced to living in one tiny house, which was spared from the gambling loss.

With that, Mother lost her job.

In the meantime, Father's father had sold his house when he moved to Hong Kong. So Father had to find another place to stay. He found a house along Serangoon Road that he rented from the Indian owner. It was a two-storey shop house. The ground floor had a large hall, and Father leased it to a dance instructor for rental income. It was a good idea that had been suggested by Mother, actually. She was the one with the business mentality. She was instrumental later on in renting out some of the spare rooms upstairs also. The house had four rooms, and they needed only one.

CHAPTER 2

Matchmaking

Arranged marriages were still an acceptable thing in the 1940s and 1950s.

Siu Yoke was fourteen years old when the Shanghai couple from whom Father and Mother had bought some furniture earlier approached them with a proposal from a gentleman from Taiwan for her hand in marriage. He was a rich businessman, according to them, and had come to Singapore on business. He was also looking for a wife. This couple had thought of Siu Yoke immediately when they found out about him. They had seen her many times when they came to deliver the furniture. The Taiwanese gentleman was twenty-nine years old.

Matchmakers made a living from gifts of appreciation when matches were successful. Gifts and tokens of appreciation were usually in the form of cash in red envelopes, which signified prosperity. These were the same kind of red envelopes that elders gave children with money in them during the Chinese Lunar New Year celebrations, with wishes of prosperity and good health. Gold or other jewelleries were sometimes also given to matchmakers, but they always preferred cash.

Tong

Usually, the girls were not revealed in person until the parents had seen the potential groom and all terms had been agreed upon. The parents would only bring photographs of the potential bride to the first meeting. Once both sides were in agreement, and the potential groom had seen the photograph of the girl, another appointment would be made, and that always included a meal. That's when the couple would be properly introduced to each other. It might seem unfair that the man would have at least seen a picture of the girl, while the girl had no idea what he would look like until that first meeting, but that's how it worked.

Siu Yoke was informed about this when Father and Mother came back from their meeting with this Taiwanese man. She felt happy and sad at the same time. She did not object to the meeting, partly because she was curious about this man, and because daughters were taught to be in filial obedience at all times.

Siu Yoke was already working as a receptionist at a local bank, and was acquainted with many other boys in the office. She was popular with all the boys in the bank because she was pretty, and so was quite an attraction to them. However, there was one particular boy whom she had grown quite fond of. He was two years older than she, slightly taller, and had a good sense of humour, which she liked. Chong Ke was always polite, and had a gentlemanly attitude towards the girls in the office. Although they had not been formally on outings as a couple, everybody considered them an item. They would go out with other colleagues for picnics and to film shows, but never alone by themselves. Everyone in the office knew they were attracted to each other, and anticipated they would end up together eventually.

When Siu Yoke told Chong Ke about this Taiwanese man that a matchmaker had arranged her to meet, the young banker fell into despair. He couldn't believe what he was hearing. As timid as he was, he wanted to confront the matchmakers, but she stopped him.

He shut his eyes in anguish. "You agreed to it?" he asked more with disbelief. than despair.

Siu Yoke only nodded sombrely.

"How could you? What about me? I thought we had a good thing going."

"It's my parent's decision," she said despondently. "Nothing I can do about it. He's my father. Anyway, it's just a first meeting. Nothing is confirmed."

"But what happens after that?" Chong Ke asked.

Siu Yoke was silent. She knew she should not be disobedient to Father and Mother's wishes, but she also had hoped they would listen to her if she felt uncomfortable with the man.

"Can you not accept it?" Chong Ke asked hopefully.

She shook her head. "Like I said, nothing is confirmed."

She left him sitting there on the park bench where they had met for the first time on their own, without the others around. Chong Ke remained, dejected.

It was not easy for Siu Yoke either. She walked away with tears welling in her eyes, but she didn't want him to see.

At the bank, it became quite awkward for both of them, which gradually affected their colleagues and, eventually, Chong Ke's work performance. Two weeks later, Siu Yoke tendered her resignation, to the disappointment of the manager. He had found her to be a very efficient and reliable employee. He tried to talk her out of it, but that was futile. She, too, had found it difficult to concentrate on her work. Her smiles and laughter in the office had become non-existent.

After the initial meeting between Father and Mother with the Taiwanese gentleman and the matchmakers, the date was set for the young couple to meet.

Siu Yoke looked so elegant in a floral blue dress specially made for the occasion, her hair tied in two pigtails and secured by two blue hair clips. Blue was her favourite colour.

The dinner was held at the Imperial Restaurant in the New World Amusement Park, a fifteen-minute walk down the road. The Taiwanese man was already there seated with the matchmakers when Father and Mother arrived with Siu Yoke. As soon as he laid eyes on her, he was mesmerized by her youthful beauty. Her face shone with an angelic glow.

He was dressed immaculately in a dark grey suit, light blue shirt, and a white bow tie. When he stood up to greet them, Siu Yoke saw he was tall. She was made to sit next to him. He spoke with such eloquence in English mixed with a splattering of Taiwanese Mandarin, both of which Father and Mother understood quite well.

Siu Yoke sat there quietly, head bowed partly in shyness but mainly because she didn't know what to talk about. It was better to keep quiet and let the others chat on. The matchmaking couple was beaming with pride and excitement, hoping for a successful deal with this beautiful match, more so because of the huge *hong pow* they expected from this wealthy Taiwanese. They were ready to discuss dowry and the date of the wedding, but Father wanted the young couple to get to know each other better before moving on to the next stage.

Although it was up to him, Father still had Siu Yoke's happiness and interest at heart. He encouraged them to get to know each other better before any decision about an engagement was made.

The Taiwanese man was very impressed with Father's approach and had much praise for him. Most other people he had met before for marriage proposals had jumped into it without much hesitation. He assumed it was because of his wealth. For himself, he was not that desperate. Father was different, he noticed.

"I think it is better for both of you to get to know each other first before further discussion about marriage," Father said and gave Siu Yoke a reassuring look that told her that her well-being and happiness came before anything else. He patted her hand, and she nodded gratefully.

"That is an excellent suggestion, Mr Pang," said the Taiwanese man. "I fully agree."

The matchmakers were disappointed. That meant their *hong pow* would be delayed. However, they still managed to say a few patronising words.

"Yes, Mr Pang. That is indeed a good suggestion," said the woman, forcing a plastic smile.

"Come. Let's toast to a new friendship," said the Taiwanese, raising his glass of red wine.

He turned to Siu Yoke to toast her. She looked at Father for permission to take the wine. He smiled and nodded, and she lifted her glass to her lips.

Nothing was mentioned about the wedding date after that.

Small talk went on the whole night, with the Taiwanese man making plenty of effort to entice Siu Yoke to come out of her shell and talk. Father and Mother noticed that and gave them the opportunity to bond. Siu Yoke, though, was not sure about everything that was happening. She didn't know if she actually wanted to get married so young. She valued her freedom, being able to go out with her friends on the weekends and holidays whenever she wanted. However, if Father and Mother had decided on it, she had to abide by it.

Asian daughters are brought up to be obedient and to be filial to their parents' wishes, she kept reminding herself.

CHAPTER 3

The Gifts

The Taiwanese gentleman, Mr Beh, had learned from the matchmakers that the house our family was staying in was a rental, since Father's photography shop at Upper Cross Street had been destroyed during the war. Upon hearing this, Mr Beh arranged to purchase the shop house and presented it as a gift for the hand of Siu Yoke. Father rejected it, saying it was not confirmed yet that Siu Yoke would be marrying him. But Mr Beh was very persistent, regardless whether they would marry or not.

"We cannot accept this," Father said. "It is not proper. We have not agreed to the engagement yet."

"It is all right, Mr Pang," Mr Beh said. "This is for Siu Yoke and you, regardless of your decision."

This was the terrace house the family was staying in when I was born in 1946. It was a two-storey shop house along Serangoon Road. There were about ten other such units along this stretch of road. Opposite the houses was an Indian temple, the Sri Mariman. Whenever there was any religious festival or activity taking place there, we could hear the sounds of drums and cymbal coming from the temple. There was some kind of festival every few months.

In one such festival, The Thaipusam, people would march out of the temple compound carrying their *kavadi*. It was a sign of repentance for all their wrongdoings over the previous year and also thanksgiving for prayers answered. The kavadi was made of two semi-circular pieces of wood or steel which were bent and attached to a cross that the devotee balanced on his shoulder. It was often decorated with peacock feathers and flowers, among other things. Some of these kavadis could weigh as much as 30 kilos, and they were carried from one temple to another, even when the temples were some distance away. In addition, some of the devotees pierced their tongues or cheeks with small spears. The spears were to remind them of one of their deities, Lord Murugan. It also prevented them from speaking and gave them great powers of endurance. Other types of kavadi involved hooks stuck into their backs that were either pulled by another bearer walking behind, or were used to hang onto the person from a decorated bullock cart. The point of the incision varied the level of pain. Other kavadi bearers had sharp thongs pieced into their bodies, their mouths, backs, and stomach. This was their way of showing repentance. Other times, the devotees would walk on hot burning coals.

The temple was surrounded by forest that was undeveloped in any way, except for the driveway leading from the main road to the temple building.

Our family stayed on the top floor of the shop house. Since Mother had rented out the ground floor to a dance instructor, there was always music and lots of laughter and dancing going on down there.

The upstairs floor was made of solid timber. I remember there was a tiny hole the size of our fifty-cent coin in the middle of this wood floor, covered with a cap. When we removed this cap, we could look down through the hole and peep at the dancers downstairs. I would watch them dance and then imitate them on my own.

The dance instructor was a handsome young man named Jimmy. I suspected that the dance students, mostly women, came there because of his good looks and not because they really wanted to learn dancing. He was also kind of a Casanova, or perhaps he had to be flirty to attract and maintain his mostly female clientele. Through the hole in the floor, sometimes I noticed that Jimmy was really taking advantage of the ladies with his amorous hands.

Mr Beh had insisted on giving this very expensive gift to our family, and the formal courting began.

Every weekend without fail, just before lunchtime, he would drive up to the front of the house in his luxurious car and wait for Siu Yoke. Occasionally, he would bring other gifts like rice, sugar, cooking oil. Both Father and Mother were overwhelmed by all this generosity, and many times they insisted that Mr Beh take the gifts back. Mr Beh would refuse. Finally Father relented, and accepted them.

Mr Beh would bring Siu Yoke to different places on different weekends. She had never had the chance to go to these many different places before, and she welcomed this opportunity. One of the places she loved going to was the Haw Par Villa located along the west coast. It was a park originally called Tiger Balm Gardens, built in 1937 by a couple of Burmese-Chinese brothers as a place for teaching traditional Chinese values. Different structures featuring Chinese mythological creatures and beings were on display, the most famous of which was the Ten Courts of Hell, which featured gruesome depictions of hell in Chinese mythology and Buddhism. This had always intrigued her the most.

Other places that Mr Beh brought Sui Yoke to were the popular tea dances at the New World Amusement Park; and the Pasir Panjang beaches along the west coast, where the water was so clear you could see fish swimming when you stood in the shallow water. Sometimes Mr Beh would drive into Johor Bahru, the southernmost tip of Malaya, for their simple yet delicious lunches. One of Siu Yoke's favourite meals was the braised duck in salted vegetable soup. Sometimes they went to Sunday afternoon tea dances at some of the day clubs.

Most Sundays, Siu Yoke would be ready when he arrived, knowing he would come around 11.30 a.m. But sometimes, she just didn't feel like going out. It became too routine, and she needed time to be on her own and think over all that had happened. It was so much so quickly.

One Sunday when Mr Beh arrived, he waited for her in his car in front of the house for almost ten minutes before Mother appeared at the door.

"Siu Yoke is not feeling well today," she said apologetically. "She started feeling sick last night. She went to bed without her dinner."

"Oh. Has she gone to see the doctor?" Mr Beh enquired, disappointed but concerned over this news.

"No. She feels that she will recover with some of the traditional Chinese herbal soup that I have boiled for her. It will help her perspire under the cover of the blanket, and then she should feel better after a while."

Mr Beh sighed. "May I see her, please?"

Mother brought him upstairs to Siu Yoke's room. She was sleeping, so Mr Beh didn't want to disturb her. He went back downstairs with Mother, telling her that he would arrange for a doctor to come by.

Later that afternoon, a man came by the house, looking for Father and Mother. He wore a white Chinese kung-fu type jacket and carried a small black bag. His hair was sleekly combed back.

"Hello. I am Dr Heng from the Heng Medical Hall down the road," he said to Father. "Mr Beh said to come by to take a look at your daughter, Siu Yoke. Is this the right place?"

Father was surprised. "Yes," he said. "Come in, please. This way." Mother had not told him about Mr Beh's visit that morning.

Father led him upstairs to Siu Yoke's room, where she was resting. He knocked on the door and entered when Siu Yoke said to come in.

She was surprised at the presence of Dr Heng. The family had not sent for him. She was sure of that because mother had already prepared the traditional Chinese herbal soup.

"Mr Beh requested for Dr Heng to come to look into your sickness," Father explained.

"Yes, Miss Pang," Dr Heng said, sitting on the stool next to her bedside. He took his stethoscope from his small black bag and stuck both ear tips into his ears. "Please sit up."

He listened to Siu Yoke's breathing from her chest and then from her back. He dipped a thermometer in her mouth for about one minute and then looked at the reading, nodding. After his examination, he put his stethoscope back in his little black bag and said, "Nothing to worry about. Just a mild temperature. Some medicine will take care of that."

"Thank you, doctor," Father said as he led Dr Heng to the door.

"Can you arrange for someone to come by to my clinic to pick up the medicine?" Dr Heng said.

"Yes," replied Father. "How much do we have to pay for all your trouble?"

"Oh. It's all taken care of by Mr Beh," Dr Heng said, and he left.

At this time, Sui Yoke's former colleagues from the office had not much chance to go out with her, because most of her weekends were already occupied with Mr Beh. However, Chong Ke had not given up.

One Sunday when Mr Beh was waiting in his car, Chong Ke was across the road, hidden from view. He waited for Siu Yoke to come out of the house. The sun was high in the sky, and it was getting hot. He stood there under the shade of the tree, perspiring with jealousy and delirium, wild thoughts running through his mind, thinking what he wanted to say to Siu Yoke when she came down.

Soon she appeared in a window, wearing her usual favourite blue dress. She saw Chong Ke standing across the road, and she stopped in her tracks. *What's he doing here?* she wondered. She didn't want a scene, so she called for Father.

Father came out of the house, crossed the road, and spoke with Chong Ke. "What are you doing here?" he asked.

"I want to see Siu Yoke, please," Chong Ke said.

"Please do not create any trouble here."

"I just want to talk to her," Chong Ke said.

"Don't waste your time and energy on this anymore, young man," Father said kindly. "It won't do anybody any good. Please just forget about her. She is going to be betrothed to another man soon."

From inside the house, Sui Yoke watched Father talking to Chong Ke, her heart heavy with sadness at the sight.

Mr Beh saw Father talking to the young man and was wondering what was happening. He got out of the car and walked over to them.

"Is there a problem, Mr Pang?" he asked as he approached. them.

Before Chong Ke could answer, Father said, "No. No problem at all. This young man is leaving now."

Father gave Chong Ke a stern look that signalled it was time for him to go. Chong Ke was about to say something when Siu Yoke appeared across the road. "Ah Pa," she called to Father.

"Siu Yoke," Chong Ke said as he made his way across the road towards her.

Surprisingly, Mr Beh was not perturbed at all. He seemed to be very calm and cool about what was taking place. He stood there in his short-sleeved yellow shirt and blue flannel slacks, looking at the young couple across the road, hands gesturing with every sentence they spoke. In fact, he seemed amused by it all.

Father apologised to Mr Beh. "I'm sorry, Mr Beh.. This young man is —"

"No need to apologise, Mr Pang," said Mr Beh. "I think I know who he is."

Father kept silent, looking at him with great admiration and respect. This was one gentleman, and he was happy that perhaps Siu Yoke would settle down with him.

"Please go, Chong Ke" Siu Yoke pleaded.

"Are you serious about this guy?" Chong Ke demanded. "I think he is too old for you. Is it because he is rich?" Chong Ke started to become aggressive, looking at the expensive car.

That made Siu Yoke upset and angry. That was an insult.

"How dare you say that?" She finally raised her voice. "Go away now. I have nothing more to say to you."

With that, Siu Yoke walked away from Chong Ke and towards Mr Beh's car, upset by the encounter.

Chong Ke refused to budge though. He stood there, lines of strain on his face as wild thoughts rushed through his mind again. He regretted deeply what he had said, but it was too late to withdraw what he had said.

Mr Beh and Father approached Chong Ke from the other side of the road.

"Hello," Mr Beh said. "My name is –"

Chong Ke interrupted him. "Don't tell me your name. I'm not interested in your name."

"Chong Ke," Father said. "Please calm down."

"Calm down?" Chong Ke said. "Calm down? When my girl is going out with another man in front of me?"

"Your girl?" said Mr Beh.

"Yes. Siu Yoke is my girlfriend," Chong Ke said.

"Is she engaged to you?" Mr Beh asked calmly. Chong Ke couldn't answer.

"Listen, my friend," Mr Beh continued. "If she wants you, she will stay with you. Evidently, it's not so. So, why don't you leave her alone?"

Chong Ke was visibly devastated. He had to accept defeat now. Was it true that Siu Yoke was no longer interested in him? He couldn't believe it. Yet, there she was, in this other man's car.

Defeated, he left grudgingly.

CHAPTER 4

The Disappointment

Siu Yoke and Mr Beh had been going out regularly, almost every weekend, for four months. They looked a perfect couple. The matchmakers were counting their 'hong pow' in their heads. They came by one day looking for Father and Mother.

"Mr and Mrs Pang. How is everything coming along now?" they asked.

What they really meant was whether any decision had been made regarding the arranged marriage between Mr Beh and Siu Yoke.

"Not yet," Father said, to their disappointment.

"It's been four months already, Mr and Mrs Pang," one of the matchmakers said. "Don't you think it's time for a decision?"

"Yes. It should be time," Father said. "We will talk to Siu Yoke later when she comes back."

Siu Yoke had enjoyed herself very much these past few months, going to some of the places she had never been to before. Mr Beh's full name was Beh Nan Chew. *Chew Ke* means Big Brother Chew in Mandarin.

"Siu Yoke," Chew Ke said on this day when they were sitting by the seaside along the Pasir Panjang beach. He had brought a basket of fruits and sandwiches for a picnic. "It's been many months now that we have been seeing each other, and I hope that you have gotten to know me better. Do you feel it's time that we discuss our marriage?"

"You have to discuss this with my parents, Chew Ke," she said.

"Yes. Of course," Chew Ke said. "But surely you also have some decision about it?"

"If my parents say it's OK, then it's OK with me too."

"You are surely such a filial daughter. I am sure you will make an equally good wife," said Chew Ke, beaming. "I will consult the fortune teller accordingly," he continued. "Can you write down your birth date and time for me so I can arrange for an auspicious date?"

He handed Siu Yoke a piece of paper from his wallet for her to write.

She wrote her birth date and time on the piece of paper and handed it to him.

He looked at it, puzzled for a moment, and asked. "Is there a mistake here, Siu Yoke?"

"What do you mean?" she asked.

"You have written your birth year as 1931. That makes you only fourteen years old." He laughed.

"Yes. That is correct. I am fourteen years old," Siu Yoke said, surprised by his remark.

For a moment, he was silent. His facial expression changed; he could not believe what he had just heard. "Siu Yoke. Please don't joke."

"It is correct," she said. "I was born in 1931. I am fourteen years old."

"But they told me you are eighteen years old," he blurted.

"Who told you that?" she asked.

"That Shanghainese couple. They told me you were eighteen years old."

Mr Beh murmured away, his face flushed with disbelief. "You are too young, Siu Yoke. I am more than twice your age. That is not right."

"I am sorry, Chew Ke. I have no idea that was what they told you," Siu Yoke said apologetically.

"We cannot go through with this marriage, Siu Yoke. I am sorry. What will people think?"

"I'm sorry, Chew Ke," she said again.

"It's OK, Siu Yoke. It's not your fault. Come. Let's pack up. I'll bring you home now."

With that, they packed up their food basket, put everything in the back of the car, and drove back to Serangoon Road, to Father's house, awkward silence all the way.

When they reached the house, Siu Yoke ran inside and up the stairs to her room without a word. Father and Mother wondered what had happened. Did the couple have a quarrel? A lovers' spat?

From her room upstairs, Siu Yoke heard muffled conversation from downstairs, the discussion between Mr Beh, Father, and Mother.

"I am sorry, Mr Beh," she heard Father say. "We had no idea they told you that. They have deceived you. I'm indeed very sorry. So we have to call off everything? But my concern now is how we can return you all the gifts that you have been so generous with."

"That is all right, Mr Pang," said Mr Beh. "I told you right from the beginning, it is for you regardless. I regret that we have to end this way. However, I have no grudge at all against you. You are not at fault."

How gracious he was. With that he left, and that was the last they saw of him.

Upstairs in her room, Siu Yoke was lost in her thoughts. She was, surprisingly, not feeling sad or happy about what had just happened. It was a bittersweet feeling she was having. It confused her. Why was she not sad or happy about it? Why was she feeling indifferent about it? Such thoughts filled her mind as she pondered over the event.

Then it dawned on her, a moment of epiphany. She had unconsciously been hoping not to be married, although she had not been unhappy going out with Mr Beh all this while. A sense of relief came upon her, and she felt immediately as if a great burden had been taken off her shoulders. She felt light.

She was just being a filial daughter, respecting the wishes of her parents. Her relationship with Mr Beh had been good, but in no way was she in love with him. It had just been an arrangement she'd had to accept. Perhaps after they had got married, she could have learned to be a good wife and would have hoped that love could develop gradually from there. Daughters were not expected to go against their parents' wishes. But now she was free again.

Would Chong Ke continue to pursue her? she wondered and immediately cast that thought aside. He wasn't her type, she decided.

That night she slept well, listening to the mellifluous sounds of crickets out in the dark that floated in.

*   *   *

Siu Yoke had decided not to go back to her job at the bank, although the manager, Mr Lim, had been contacting her, asking if she would consider going back. She didn't want to have to face Chong Ke and the others after what had happened. She would stay home and help Mother with her housework and other chores.

She did miss going out with her former co-workers though.

However, news of her engagement and marriage being called off reached them. Now that she was once again single and free, they started arranging outings with her. So on weekends now, she and her friends went to the beaches and the movies once again. Sometimes they would board sampans, those little wooden boats operated by a single boatman, who for a mere ten cents would take them out to the smaller islands around Singapore. They would spend the whole day swimming, playing games, and having a great time together, just like before. However, this time round, Chong Ke did not join them. She learned that he had also resigned from the bank not too long after she left. Perhaps she might consider going back to work in the bank, her friends asked.

Suddenly, she regretted leaving her job at the bank again. Would her manager, Mr Lim, accept her if she were to ask for her old job back?

She pondered going back to the bank and seeing her former colleagues again. Only a few understood her and her situation at home, friends she had been going out with after she left the bank. People like Diana, who worked at the counter. Diana would always stand in whenever Siu Yoke needed to go to the washroom. There was Siew Lan, the remittance clerk, always so chirpy and bubbly; and Vivian, the secretary to the manager, who would offer to buy lunch for her whenever she couldn't go out because she had to finish her dateline jobs.

But what about the others? Chong Ke no longer worked there, but what would he say if he found out? Anyway, it was none of his business anymore, since they were no longer an item.

What about Mr Lim, the manager? Would he accept her back if she applied for her old job, or any other job that might be available? After all, he had invited her back to her job the last time, but that was a long time ago. The job would have been taken over by somebody else by now. All right, she would approach Mr Lim for a job. Failing that, she would try elsewhere.

Yes, she would. Soon, she was interviewed again by the manager, who was so eager to have her back, and within days she was back at the bank.

CHAPTER 5

Father Dies

Father had been sick for a while. He had been coughing and running out of breath so often. The doctors couldn't do much for him, except feed him more medicine. A year after he was diagnosed with tuberculosis, he passed away in 1948 at the age of forty-four. Siu Yoke was devastated. So sad that she could not eat for days, and she lost so much weight. Mother tried to console her, but it didn't work and she too was deeply saddened by her husband's passing. It was a long time before they gradually got over it.

After Father died, Mother took over running the family affairs. She was still a young lady in her forties. She was still good looking and very capable, and suddenly she was also available. Many suitors had their eyes on her after Father passed on, but she totally ignored them. She had no time for them. She was much more interested in getting food on the table for the family.

When Father was still alive, they had rented out one room on the upper floor of our terrace house to a lady who worked as a dance hostess. She didn't bother the family too much, coming in and going out quietly and paying her rent on time. She had a man who did come by occasionally, who disappeared into her room for hours. He was her sugar daddy.

Then Mother began renting out the other spare rooms in the house. There were four rooms altogether. She had no need for so many rooms. She even erected partitions in the bigger rooms, making them into two smaller rooms, and rented them. This way, our house had six rooms instead of four.

All the new tenants turned out to be ladies of the night. Mother was a shrewd business lady and knew where the rental market was. It was from this kind of tenant that good money would be made, and she made sure they always paid in advance before the month was due. Anytime they skipped a payment, they were out. That's how tough Mother was. All the tenants knew that, and they wouldn't risk being thrown out into the streets.

Now that all the rooms in the main part of the house were let out, Mother had a room specially constructed at the back of the house for Siu Yoke and I, away from these tenants – and away from the prying eyes of the visitors of the tenants. I was only three years old, and was too young to understand anything. But she took care of me. She couldn't leave me alone at home unattended.

In spite of her living in the room at the back of the house, the male visitors still had to go by her room to the toilet behind the kitchen. In those days, toilets were at the backs of houses. The stench of urine always lingered in the air outside the room, sometimes becoming so suffocating that she had to get out of the house for fresh air.

Other times when the male visitors went to the toilet, they would peek into her room. Sometimes they made faces at her, which annoyed and scared her at the same time. She began to live in constant fear and anxiety.

One day one of the male guests poked his head into her doorway while she was in her bed reading.

"Hello," he said. "Why are you locked up here? Have you been a naughty girl?" He leered at her.

She jumped out of her bed and rushed to shut the door, but he put his foot there, preventing the door from shutting. He reached for her hand, and she screamed. Moments later, one of the tenants came rushing to the back and saw the man trying to get into her room. She rushed up and pulled him by his shirt out of the room. She gave him a slap so hard, he almost fell down.

"How dare you?" she said. "Don't you touch her again. She's not in this business."

She was furious. Or maybe she was jealous. She pulled him by the ear, back to her room. There was a lot of shouting and screaming coming from her room, but then after a while, there was silence.

Siu Yoke sat on her bed, trembling with fear. Oh, how she wished she could get out of that place. Ever since Mother started letting out rooms to these ladies, life had been nerve-racking. Sometimes, the ladies came back from work drunk. Sometimes, they vomited in the hallway on their way to their rooms, stinking the whole place. The servants that Mother hired to take care of the place didn't stay long either. They quit after a few weeks. They could not take the nonsense from these women.

Her friends from the bank and other friends that she had stopped visiting her. They felt uneasy being seen in a place like this. Siu Yoke similarly was feeling extremely uneasy and shameful to be living in an environment like this. However, Mother was oblivious to all of this. She was too busy thinking and arranging all kinds of business ventures to notice. She seemed not to have any time for the family anymore. She had brought food for the table for all. That was good enough.

Siu Yoke had to do something about this. She did not want to live like this anymore. She had to get out of this place. But where could she go? Who could she turn to? If Father were still alive, this would not be happening. But alas, he was no more there for them.

She had cousins that she would turn to, to voice her grievances. Violet was one of them, from Father's side. She was sympathetic but only had comforting words. More than that, she could not do anything. But Siu Yoke had always found comfort in Violet's company. The two of them, with other cousins and friends, would go on long trips upcountry into Malaya for days, for her to get away from home. Every time she was away, Sui Yoke felt great relief and never wanted to think about home. Each time, when it came to the end of the outings and it was time for us to go home, she dreaded it and wished she could slow down the clock, so that her return home would be delayed, or not happen at all.

What was happening? Why did she have to live like this? Maybe she should have married Mr Beh back then. Then this could be avoided.

She spent sleepless nights in bed, fearing that any moment a man might intrude into her room.

Her embarrassment did not end there. In the office, she noticed her colleagues had been avoiding her, leaving her out when they went for their lunches. Their occasional outings were now arranged without her too.

One day, Vivienne, one of her colleagues who had been feeling sorry for her, extended an invitation for her to go boating that coming weekend. Siu Yoke knew she'd been invited out of pity and politely turned Vivienne down.

"I have to take care of house work this weekend," she said. "Thanks for the invitation, anyway."

However, Vivienne knew that she was just using work as an excuse not to join them. She felt sorry for Siu Yoke.

"Look, Siu Yoke," she said. "I'm sorry if we haven't been including you in our outings of late. We've been talking about it for a while, and we felt that it was really unkind of us to leave you out like that. We've always enjoyed your company, and we want you to come back and join us again, just like before."

Siu Yoke looked at her, fighting back the tears that were welling up. "Let me think about it," she said. She was strong and didn't need any sympathy from anyone, or so she thought.

She decided that it would be good to be back with the group, as it would give her a chance to escape from home, to be away from all the perverts on the weekends and holidays when there was no work and she had to stay home.

She wondered when she would be able to get away from Mother and the horrible home environment. She had been brought up to observe filial piety, and she had battled her thoughts of rebelling against Mother by running away. She also could not imagine leaving her little brother behind, defenceless. Violet knew her thoughts and discouraged her from them, telling her not even to think about such things.

"You have no idea how scared I am every time I'm home, Violet. Especially when I'm all alone in my room only with my little brother," Siu Yoke said

"Why don't you tell Aunty how you feel, and maybe she will do something about it," Violet said.

"Like what?" Siu Yoke retorted. "She is hardly home, so I have no opportunity to talk to her."

"Well, the next time you see her, take the opportunity," Violet said. "She has to come home occasionally, doesn't she?"

Violet was right, Siu Yoke thought. Mother had to come back from time to time, if not for anything but to collect the rents from the ladies. Siu Yoke just had to be there when she was. So she had to wait. But to her disappointment, most times when Mother came back, Siu Yoke was at work; and by the time Siu Yoke returned home from work, Mother had left. This went on for months.

One day while they were at the Pasir Panjang beach, enjoying a swim, Violet said,

"Siu Yoke, why don't you move in with me?"

Siu Yoke gave her a long look, which made Violet think she was considering the possibility.

"Don't need to hesitate," she said. "Just go pack some stuff that you need and move in with me. It's not long term, of course. I understand. I believe you really need to ease your mind and give yourself a chance to detoxify all the bad feelings that you've been accumulating all this time."

"OK. That is a good idea." Siu Yoke was so grateful for Violet's suggestion and her show of love.

So, right after the swim, they went off to Siu Yoke's home and packed up as much as they could. While they were there, Violet could see the uneasiness that was creeping up Siu Yoke as they walked past the ladies' rooms to get to the back of the house, where Siu Yoke's room was. There were some men hanging around the air well, smoking and chatting. As the girls walked past, they gave wolf calls and whistled at them. Violet understood more clearly why Siu Yoke really needed to get away from this place called home. It didn't feel like home at all.

It didn't look like a proper home. It didn't feel like a home. It clearly came to her what kind of a place Mother was running.

They hurried into Siu Yoke's room and packed up as much as she needed – work clothes and going-out clothes, toothbrush, powder, makeup. As fast as they came, they hurried off with me.. They were glad that when they came out of Siu Yoke's room, the men were no longer around. They had gone back into their respective ladies' rooms.

*   *   *

We stayed at Violet's place longer than they had expected. Violet had insisted we stayed there as long as she wanted. Siu Yoke was relieved to have this retreat away from the unholy environment of home.. Violet had worked as a ticket seller at the Odeon Cinema. She would smuggle Siu Yoke and I in whenever there was a show that she thought Siu Yoke would be interested in.

Violet was a small girl, two years older than Siu Yoke, and their bond was so close that people usually mistook them for sisters. Their fellowship and kinship was deep, with an intimate understanding of each other's habits and character. They had grown up together since they were young.

Some nights, they would chat into the early hours of the morning, forgetting that they had to work the next day. Sui Yoke had told Mother's servants that we were staying at Violet's in case Mother came looking for us. It did not happen. Mother had become a busy woman, putting all her attention on her business interests in Johor Bahru, a small district at the southern tip of the Malay Peninsula, about an hour's bus ride across the causeway. She was ambitious, and her friends could see that. They took advantage of her lack of experience and gullibility. They introduced her to all sorts of business ventures that she had no experience with at all, but they assured her they would give her all the assistance and help she needed to run those businesses. They had the experiences but not the necessary finances, so they said it was a good collaboration for them to team up. Mother agreed. She invested a huge sum of money into the trading business that her friends started. They were to import timber from Indonesia and sell it to government projects for expanding the township of Johor Bahru. It had great potential for expansion into the other Malay states.

Mother was thrilled. She was looking forward to being rich and financially independent. Because of that, she spent all her time in Johor Bahru and never got home to check on things. The tenants took advantage of her absence. They started subletting their rooms to other women for short periods of time and collecting rentals for that. More men came. They were a rowdy lot; uncouth, unkempt, dirty, and spewing obscenities with every sentence they spoke. Some started gambling with small black strips of paper cards called Twelve Sticks or, in the Chinese dialect, 'Chap Ji Kee'. Each player would hold up to twelve of these cards, and that was the reason for the name. It was similar to another tile game called mah-jong, except that this was in paper strip form. Whenever the game grew intense, the noise level grew as well. The house started to look like a den for thieves. Nobody told Mother about it.

Siu Yoke definitely was not in a position to do anything. When she went home to pick up some fresh changes of clothes, she was shocked to witness all this. She was so ashamed of even being there. What was happening? What was going on? How could Mother allow this to continue? Didn't she know? These thoughts raced through her mind as she silently but quickly grabbed her clothes. As she stepped out of her room and hurried out of the house, she felt the men's lustful glares.

It was getting out of hand. Mother should be told about it. But where was Mother now? She would be absent for many months and then come back, usually without any prior notice, just to collect the rents and then disappear again. This went on for a long time..

When Siu Yoke returned to Violet's home, she relayed what she had seen. She was so ashamed about it, but she knew Violet would understand. She had always been a good listener and counsellor.

"You have to tell Aunty," Violet said. "Otherwise she will not know, and this will continue."

"I wish I had the opportunity, Violet," Siu Yoke replied, "but you know that Mother is hardly home, and I don't get to see her. I won't know when she will be back."

"I think you have to go home and wait for her, so that you can catch her when she returns."

This suggestion gave Siu Yoke the creeps, knowing what it was like back home with all the men and the new unknown tenants. Some of those new tenants had even thought that Siu Yoke was in their kind of business when she went home for her things. It was unthinkable to even consider going back; and even worse, to stay there for an indefinite period of time, just waiting for Mother to come home.

"I can't do that," she said, shaking her head, her voice cracking with despondency.

Violet felt her distress. After a while, she said, "I'll go stay with you. I'll keep you company until Aunty comes back."

Siu Yoke was touched by Violet's kind offer, knowing that her cousin was equally uneasy to be in that house too.

"No," she said. "You don't have to do that, Violet. I will manage." She told herself that she ought to be able to stand on her own. She just needed to bring out the strength and courage that could be latent in her.

"Are you very sure about that, Siu Yoke?" Violet asked.

Siu Yoke forced a nod.

"OK. But the moment you feel any need for help, just call, and I will be there, Sis." They sometimes addressed each other as Sister.

"Thank you," Siu Yoke said. She could hardly hide her fear as she spoke.

CHAPTER 6

From a Cat to a Lioness

We moved back home after staying at Violet's for almost three months. Moving back to Serangoon Road was not easy for Siu Yoke. The house she'd grown up in had lost its respectability. The house where she had shared so many wonderful memories with Father had lost its shine. She felt sad, disgusted, and shameful to be under the same roof with these undesirable people. But what could she do? It was Mother's choice of business, and it was what brought food to the table every week and month. What would Father think if he knew what was happening to the house now? She knew Mother had no choice because she had no other skills, and this was probably the easiest way to make a living.

Siu Yoke waited impatiently for the day that she would see Mother coming home. She ticked the dates off the calendar that hung on the wall, counting the days as she did. The servants were of no help at all. They had been won over with the tips they received from the women tenants and their men friends every time they did a chore for them, like running over to the nearest coffee shop for cigarettes, coffee, tea, beer, or food, and washing their dirty laundry. The tips were no small change either. It kept the maidservants so busy, they did not have the time to take care of our needs – to cook our meals, do our laundry, or clean the house, which they were hired to do.

When Mother comes home, they'll get fired for sure, Siu Yoke thought. After many days of observing their behaviour and how they didn't do their duties, she could take it no longer. It was not like they didn't know Siu Yoke was there. It was not like they didn't know their jobs. They were so blatantly ignoring her presence as well as her requests for food to be prepared and the laundry to be done. She voiced her dissatisfaction to them about their lack of responsibility and chided them for being so mercenary. To her dismay, they scoffed at her, telling her she was in no position to tell them what to do. That made Siu Yoke really furious, and she assured them in no uncertain terms that she would report them to Mother when the opportunity presented itself. They just laughed in her face.

"Go fix your own dinner, 'Siew Che'," one of them jeered at her. *Siew Che* in Cantonese means Mistress or lady of the house. It was a respectful greeting when addressed by a servant honourably and in its proper sense to the lady of the house. On the other hand, it could be used sarcastically to show disrespect to another.

"We are making more money here than what your mother is paying us," said the other one. "So you can tell her to keep her job."

What kind of talk was that? Siu Yoke thought. What kind of disrespectful behaviour was that? She suddenly felt a rush of blood come over her head, blinding her momentarily. They had no respect for the owner of this place, it seemed. Something really had to be done. She should stand up for her right as the owner's daughter.

With all of her built-up anger, Siu Yoke summoned enough courage and shouted at them, "Since you are not interested in the job we have given you, you are both fired. I insist that you leave our property now. This instant."

She spoke loudly enough for everyone else to hear. She wanted even the tenants to hear this. She shocked herself too, as she had never been so loud and outspoken.

What's come over me? she thought.

She couldn't believe she had lowered herself to such a level that she'd shout at anyone. However, since she had done it, there was no backing out. Her eyes grew fearfully big as she glared at the two maidservants. Pointing fingers straight into their faces, she demanded, "Are you going to leave now, or do I have to call the authorities?"

The servants were taken aback. This was the first time they had seen Siu Yoke like this, her face flushed with tearful anger. They couldn't believe it and gave each other looks of surprise mixed with fear and disbelief. This they had not expected.

When they didn't move, Siu Yoke said, "I said now. What are you waiting for?"

"Ma'am, are you sure about this?" one asked timidly, in a respectful tone. But it was too late. They had crossed the line.

Siu Yoke felt sick to her stomach that she had to deal with these kinds of people. Hiding her trembling fear, she said, "Yes. I want you to leave now."

She turned to go back to her room, but before closing the door, she faced them again. "When I come out, I don't want to see any of you here."

With that she went into her room.

Once inside her room with the door closed, Siu Yoke broke down, trembling and crying with fear and disgust over what had just taken place. She couldn't contain the disgust that was overpowering her. She tried to muffle her sobs with a pillow. It was not like her to lose her cool like that. It was not like her to chide anybody like that. It was not something she was proud of.

She wanted to call Violet but didn't know what to say. She wondered if she had done the right thing. Maybe she should call Violet to let her know what had happened. Violet would be able to advise her, tell her if what she'd done was right or not.

No. She should not call Violet. Whatever Violet said would make no difference. After all, it was done. Her immediate task was to make sure the maidservants left and did not take anything that didn't belong to them. She jumped off the bed, dried her tears, and ran out of her bedroom, wondering if she would see the maidservants around.

She didn't see either of them anywhere. She walked into the kitchen, but they were not there. Looking around, she felt nothing was missing. She walked into the hall. Nothing missing there. The vases and Father's antique collections were there. She went downstairs. She looked into every room and closet. She looked out the door to see if she could see them walking away, or perhaps hanging around outside. No. They were nowhere to be seen. All the while, the tenants were watching her, this time with much respect.

With a sigh of relief, she battled to hold back the tears. Thank goodness. She didn't think she would know what next to do if she had found them still hanging around in the house.

She walked back upstairs to her room, her mind filled with thoughts of what to tell Mother and wondering how Mother would react when she learned that she had fired both maidservants. Mother would understand. After all, she was her daughter. Although they had never been close, they were still a family. All mothers should stand by their children's decisions, especially when it came to protecting the family's interests.

The women tenants and their men friends became unusually quiet after that, having witnessed a timid housecat grow into a lion. They wondered if this was a new boss lady in the making, taking charge of the place and taking business into her hands. Individually, they felt a certain respect for this girl, whom they had watched coming in and going out over the years, minding her own business, and always staying in the shadows. She had grown from a cat to this roaring lion.

Unbeknownst to them, Siu Yoke felt sick to the bones at what she'd done. She still felt a quivering tremble as she lay in her bed that night, having gone to bed without her dinner. She was not hungry.

Now, she had the responsibility of cleaning the house, doing the laundry, and making our meals. She would not want to have anything to do with the tenants, and would not serve them like the maids. But if Mother wanted her to collect the weekly and monthly rent, she would. After all, that was why they had rented out the rooms, even though it wasn't her ideal business.

She would now wait for Mother to come back. Then she would explain to her why the maidservants had to be fired. Mother would understand.

For the next few weeks, Siu Yoke prepared our meals.. At times we would eat out at the coffee shop just around the corner. It was more convenient to eat out, since it was much more work cooking for just two persons. Eventually, we ate out for every meal. She only did the laundry once a week, as she hardly wore many different clothes, since she had not been going out with her friends as often as before. She would have gotten some food for me in the morning before she went to work, and I would know how to help myself to it.

The tenants were showing some respect for her. Every time they passed her room to go to the toilet, they greeted her, which they had never done before. Sometimes on their way in or out of the house, if they saw her, they would give her a respectful nod or greeting. Out of courtesy, Siu Yoke would either nod in return or say some polite things. She did not respond to their men friends when they greeted her. She wanted to make sure they didn't get any wrong ideas. That didn't stop the men from saying hello each time they saw her.

One by one, the women began paying their rent to Siu Yoke, which they had never done before. They had waited until Mother came back and demanded it from them. All this came as a pleasant surprise to Siu Yoke. She didn't mind receiving the money, as she was running low. The last time Mother gave her some pocket money was about four months ago.

Many weeks went by, but there was no news of Mother coming home. Siu Yoke began to feel uneasy all over again. Why was Mother like this? Didn't she feel she had a family to come home to, even if the one family was her daughter and a young son? Siu Yoke didn't understand. Did Mother love her at all? Maybe she was adopted. All kinds of thoughts flooded her mind, just like each time she felt lost. She would harbour all kinds of unwanted thoughts.

No, she could not be an adopted child. She looked like Father too much to be adopted, she consoled herself. So she banished that thought. Could it be that Mother had wanted a son instead? That could be a possibility. It was a time when boys were favoured over baby girls. She hoped she was wrong. She would ask Father, but alas, he was not there for her anymore. If she asked Mother, she didn't think she would get an honest answer. She just had to live with that thought. Maybe one day she would find out. Maybe one day. But for now, she had to continue to fend for herself.

CHAPTER 7

Mother Returns Home

Siu Yoke had not been sleeping well the last few weeks, since the incident with the servants. She was having second thoughts about what she'd done and felt bad about it. It was not like her to be like that. She couldn't forgive herself and wondered if she should find them to apologise. She had been tossing in bed during the night, restless over that incident.

Staying alone in that room with me was not very comfortable either. Although the lady tenants were not giving her any problems, the different men that came and went at all hours continued to give her the creeps. Some of these visitors got quite rowdy at times – drunk, smelly, and noisy. The ubiquitous stench of cigarette smoke, liquor, and urine was overpowering at times.

Sometimes when she finally was able to fall asleep, she would be awakened by the loud laughter of the tenants and their guests; as they scurried in and out of their respective rooms; sometimes by angry shouts and quarrels that broke the stillness of the dark early hours of the morning. Covering her face with pillows did not help.

One particularly bad night, she decided that when the morning light came, she would confront the tenants about their guests. They would listen to her, now that she had won their respect. Yes, that's what she would do. She gradually fell back to sleep, in the midst of her struggling thoughts. Rest came but not so easily. Still it came as she was overpowered by her tiredness. However, when daylight arrived, she procrastinated about her intended action. She couldn't make herself do it. She already felt bad about firing the servants. She didn't want to have to deal with this new problem and then later regret it. What if the tenants ganged up on her or moved out totally?

That thought actually put a smile on her face. That would be the best thing that could happen. She would be able to live a normal life again. She would be able to have her friends come over like any other normal girl her age. How nice that would be.

Even as she relished that thought, her smile disappeared as her second thought came: it would be disastrous for Mother. No, she mustn't let that happen. Mother would be upset. Very upset. This was her business, her entire life. She would have to let Mother take care of the tenant problems when she returned. Siu Yoke had to wait. But when would Mother come home?

Siu Yoke was at a loss again. She was caught between wanting to get out of this miserable place and being a filial daughter to a mother. Deep in her heart, she suspected that Mother did love her. She just was not able to show it the way Father had. Father had always been there for her. Father had always watched out for her, even when she was working in the bank. He had always been there to give her advice, such as who he felt would be good for her as a friend and who he felt she should avoid. He would watch for her return whenever she went out with her friends on the weekends. When she was much younger and still in school, he would take time off from work to help her with her schoolwork. It was he who came to brush the dust from her dress when she fell playing with friends outside the house. It was he who dressed her up nicely for her photo shoots, the ones he displayed proudly in the front of his shop.

Mother was not like that. She was not the expressive type. She had never been as attentive as Father. Oh, how Siu Yoke missed Father. Those brief memories always came up when she started comparing what was happening now with when Father was still around. She fought back the tears each time such memories popped up. She didn't want to think about it anymore, though. She had to move on. Be strong.

Laughter and loud talking in the hall interrupted her thoughts. That voice. Siu Yoke rushed to the door, her heart pounding, and peered through the open curtain. Through the half-open door, she saw the tenants gathering around and looking at some clothes and dresses that had been spread over the long dining table and some of the chairs. They were admiring the displays, murmuring oohs and wows and wrestling with one another to touch the beautiful dresses and other clothes.

Mother had come home, and she had brought all these nice things with her. Yes. Mother was indeed a businesswoman. She always brought merchandise back from her trips. Siu Yoke was filled with relief, anger, and anxiety.

Relief because finally Mother had come home. Anger because she did not look for her children first as most mothers would when they returned home from a long trip. Anxiety because she didn't know how Mother would react when she heard the news about the maidservants.

Siu Yoke stood in the doorway, contemplating what to do. Should she wait for Mother to be done with her business with the tenants before she approached her? Or should she go ahead and interrupt her?

She decided to wait. After all, she had waited for so many months, what was another few minutes?

Siu Yoke went back to her room and lay down on her bed whilst waiting for mother to finish with her business. Besides, she was tired. Before long she dozed off, her eyes too heavy. Sleep was a pleasant relief.

It was dark outside when she next opened her eyes. She turned the table lamp on and looked at the clock hanging on the wall. It was eight o'clock. She had slept for over three hours and had missed dinner. Suddenly, she remembered Mother and the tenants looking at clothes in the dining room. Was that a dream, or had Mother come home? She was unsure now.

She ran out of the room and into the hall. The ladies were already busy with their business, men coming in and out of their rooms, some half naked to Siu Yoke's disgust. The smell of beer and cigarette smoke filled the air, choking her again. She tried to walk as fast as she could down this corridor to the stairs. She expected Mother would be in the kitchen downstairs. Before she entered the kitchen, she heard voices coming from there. The voices sounded familiar. One of them belonged to Mother, she was sure. She tried to make out the other voice. It sounded so familiar, but she could not place a face to it.

As she neared the doorway to the kitchen, the talking stopped. The visitors were the Shanghainese matchmaking couple. The familiar voice belonged to the man. They greeted Siu Yoke cordially. She looked at Mother expectantly.

"Ma," Siu Yoke said, greeting Mother.

"Ah Yoke you missed your dinner," Mother said. "You must be tired. Go get your food now for yourself and Ah Tong. It is in the food cabinet. There are vegetables and chicken, enough for a growing girl like you. Have your food outside in the living room."

Siu Yoke obediently collected the food, dishing rice from the rice pot on the stove, and went to the living room, just outside the kitchen area. She went into the room to pick me up. While we ate, she could still hear Mother and the Shanghainese couple talking, only this time in hushed tones. She could hardly make out what they were saying. She was hungry, so she concentrated on her food. Before she finished, Mother was escorting the Shanghainese couple to the front door. They said their goodbyes and left. Mother came back to where Siu Yoke and I were still eating. Mother sat across the table from her and poured herself a cup of tea.

"How is the food?" Mother asked.

"It is delicious, Ma."

"Good," Mother said. "Don't forget to wash up the dishes after you're done."

"Ma," Siu Yoke called as Mother walked away.

Mother turned and looked at her. "What is it?"

Siu Yoke hesitated, trying to find the right words to say. "The maidservants ..." she started but didn't know how to continue.

"I know," Mother said. "The women told me."

"I'm sorry, Ma."

"It's all right," Mother said and walked off towards the front of the house. Then she stopped as if remembering something. She turned around and said, "Someone just asked for your hand in marriage."

She waited for a response, which did not come. Siu Yoke continued eating her food, head bowed.

Mother walked back to her and sat down in the chair across the table. She looked at Siu Yoke, waiting. Siu Yoke kept eating her food.

Thoughts were rushing through her mind: memories of her childhood; the Japanese war; her dates with Mr Beh; the quarrel she had with Chong Ke; and most of all, Father. She remembered posing for him in his works. He was so proud of her, and she had adored him in return. She remembered her outings with Violet and with her office colleagues. All these came flashing back in a moment that took no longer than two seconds, all of them as vivid and clear as if they had happened just yesterday.

She fought back her tears as she thought of Father. What would he do if he were there now? What would his decision be? He would allow her to decide for herself, she was sure, just as he had done with Mr Beh.

"You think about it," Mother said. "The boy is from a wealthy family. You will be well taken care of."

Siu Yoke spoke after a long pause. "Yes, Ma. I will think about it." She was relieved that Mother was giving her the chance to think about it. Could that mean she was in a position to make her own decision?

CHAPTER 8

The Fight

Sleep would not come that night. Siu Yoke tossed and turned in bed, struggling to sleep while unable to stop thinking about what Mother had said earlier that night. Siu Yoke struggled with the decision to accept or oppose Mother's desire for her to be married, especially to someone she hadn't met. Why was this happening again? She suspected it came from the Shanghainese couple Mother had been talking with. Why did they keep coming back to taunt her with such proposals? In the case of Mr Beh, Father had given her the opportunity to get to know Mr Beh and for her to make the final decision. Would Mother do the same? She didn't know. Mother hadn't said anything like that.

Her thoughts were interrupted by angry shouting outside her room in the hall that led to the tenants' rooms. She heard a woman shouting vulgarities, and then a man yelled back with more vulgarities. Then there were running footsteps, the sound of someone being slapped, cries, and more shouting. Things were thrown. She could hear them breaking. More slapping, a woman's cry again, then a door slammed loudly.

All this commotion woke Mother up. She came out of her room and said at the top of her voice, "Stop all this nonsense or I'll call the police!"

That did not help. The fighting continued, with the man punching and slapping Ah Lan, one of the tenants. She fought back with all her might, scratching and biting like a cat, screaming curses, even though she was bleeding from her mouth. She was slim built and only about twenty years old, so she could not withstand the man's blows easily.

Mother went to intervene, trying to stop the man from hitting Ah Lan more, but she was not strong enough. He pushed her aside, and she toppled over a chair and fell to the ground. Siu Yoke rushed out of her room to help Mother to her feet.

"Get back into your room!" Mother shouted. "Go back into your room now. Don't get involved."

"But, Ma," Siu Yoke protested.

"Get back into your room right now." Mother pushed away Siu Yoke's extended hand.

Taken aback by this rejection, Siu Yoke backed away. She walked back into her room and shut the door behind her.

I have to get out of this place. I really have to, she thought as she sat on her bed, angry and frightened. Mostly angry.

Soon, she heard a siren coming to a stop in front of the house.

"Buka pintu. Ini police," the police shouted in their Malaysian language. Most policemen were Malays, with few other races, like the Chinese or the Indians, being the minority.

So, someone had called the police. The cacophony must have disturbed the neighbours. It didn't matter who had called them. It was a relief they had come.

Mother went to open the front door. Siu Yoke heard loud talking and some more shouting.

"Ok. Everybody diam (shut up)," the sergeant shouted as he came up the stairs with his troop.

All the tenants went into their respective rooms with their "guests," except Ah Lan and the angry man who had been assaulting her. The police officer who was in charge, Sergeant Ahmad, pulled him aside and started questioning him, while a lady police officer took Ah Lan to another corner to take her statement. A medical attendant had come along, and she tended to Ah Lan's wounds.

There was a lot of confusion, and accusations and counteraccusations were made until Siu Yoke couldn't make out who was at fault or what had actually happened. Mother was in the midst of all these people and also had to give a statement.

Siu Yoke watched all this through the half-parted curtain at her doorway. This was the first time she had witnessed something like this in her home. This was not the kind of environment she would want to continue living in. This was not home. At least, not the home she had grown up in when Father was still around.

What had Mother turned this place into? Siu Yoke's friends wouldn't visit her. Even when Violet came, she was not comfortable and wanted to leave as fast as she could, although she never liked leaving Siu Yoke alone. It really sickened her.

Siu Yoke's desire to get out of the place grew stronger as she lay sleepily on her bed that night. Sleep crept over her as she lay there, exhausted from all the tension.

That night she had a bad dream, but she could only vaguely remember what it was about the following morning. It had been a nightmare about staying in that house. She had looked at the outside world through prison bars instead of through a normal window.

That nightmare reinforced her desperate desire to get out of the house, to be as far away as possible and not associated with the place anymore. She had dreaded coming home early after work, but for her young brother.

All of a sudden, she remembered about the marriage proposal. Somebody had asked for her hand in marriage, Mother had said. She was sure it had been proposed by that Shanghainese couple she'd seen talking to Mother. Should she consider accepting the proposal? This would be her chance to get out of this place if she accepted it. But she didn't want it to look like she was accepting it out of desperation. She also wanted to check out the boy and his family.

She would wait for the right time to inform Mother of her decision. Mother would be pleased, but she wouldn't want Mother to think that her decision had anything to do with her desire to get out of the house. She would consult with Violet before speaking to Mother. Yes, that's what she would do. Gradually, sleep overcame her.

CHAPTER 9

The Preparation

"Are you very sure about that?" Violet asked in between mouthfuls of papaya and pineapple when they met two days later for lunch.

"That's one of the ways I can get away from that horrible place," Siu Yoke said.

"But you have not met the boy or his family," Violet said.

"They will arrange for that first. After I meet the boy and his family, then I will decide." Siu Yoke was almost trying to convince herself rather than Violet.

"Is that how it works?" Violet asked with concern. Siu Yoke was silent. "You have to think very carefully about this," Violet went on. "Marriage is for life. It's not like playing house. Remember your engagement with Mr Beh?"

"That was a long time ago," said Siu Yoke. "And he was a nice man."

"Except you were too young for him. Or he was too old for you." Violet grinned, hoping to make Siu Yoke smile. It didn't work.

Siu Yoke looked at her, her eyes brimming with tears. Violet was more than a cousin. She was a very good friend and confidante.

"I have to get out of this frying pan," Siu Yoke said. She broke down in tears, sobbing quietly at the thought of Father once again. He would not have let this happen if he were still around. "I'll meet the boy and his family first," she said, controlling her crying. "Then I'll decide."

Violet looked at her with concern. "OK, Sis. Just meeting the boy and his family is no harm. But make your decision very, very carefully."

Siu Yoke was relieved to have spoken her thoughts and hear what Violet had said. She felt more confident now about her decision. She would talk to Mother about meeting the boy and his family, and Mother would speak to the matchmakers.

What would the boy and his family think of her if they knew the sort of environment she was living in? They must not know. Would they still accept her if they did find out? It wasn't her doing, they should know. It was Mother, not her. She would explain that to them if they found out.

She would talk to Mother about her decision first, and then she would wait for the meeting to be arranged. Her thoughts began to run wild again as she imagined what it would be like to be married, to begin a family of her own, and – most importantly – to be out of the horrible place she used to call home.

Would Father approve of her marriage decision? Would he be happy for her? What would he say?

It didn't matter. Father was no longer there. That was reality and she had to move on. Father would want her to do that.

*   *   *

The next morning, Siu Yoke woke up to the sound of chirping birds and to bright sunshine. It was a nice breezy morning, and the air was cool and calm. She was enveloped by a surprising sense of calm and serenity. Nothing could spoil her day today. She wanted to start off the day with so much expectation, and she felt nothing could spoil it for her. It was such a nice feeling, a rich feeling of peacefulness, free of any anxiety. She felt good.

Today she would talk to Mother after work about meeting with the boy and his family.

"Mother," she called as she came out of her room and walked towards the kitchen, where she expected Mother to be at this time in the morning. Mother was not there. She headed for the front of the house, calling as she did, but there was no response.

Siu Yoke started for the staircase to go downstairs. Perhaps Mother was in the kitchen down there.

She was, sitting at the kitchen table, having her coffee and breakfast.

"Come, have something to eat," Mother said when she saw Siu Yoke.

Siu Yoke sat down on the opposite side of the table and helped herself to the bread. She spread jam and butter on the bread, and then poured herself a cup of coffee.

She pondered whether this was the right time to tell Mother about her decision to meet the boy. How would Mother react to that? She should be happy, shouldn't she?

"Ma," she started, and then took a sip of her coffee.

Mother looked up from her breakfast, not saying a word. She just stared at Siu Yoke with an enquiring look on her face. Siu Yoke stared into her coffee cup, frowning as she struggled to decide if she should say what she came for.

After a long pause, Mother spoke. "What is it, Yoke?"

"I ..." Siu Yoke could not bring herself to say what she wanted to say. "It's nothing, Mother."

Siu Yoke sat there, perplexed. She hated herself for it. Why couldn't she bring herself to speak up? Why was she so capricious?

"If you have nothing to say, then I have," Mother said. "Remember I told you that somebody has approached me for your hand in marriage?"

Siu Yoke almost stopped breathing. Mother was going to bring the subject up herself. "Yes," she said.

"I have agreed to have a meeting with the boy and his family."

"When?" Siu Yoke asked, hiding her excitement.

"As soon as I have spoken to the Shanghai couple. They are the ones who are introducing us. I will let you know as soon as it has been arranged."

Siu Yoke was silent, forgetting her coffee as she was lost in her thoughts again. Her immediate problem of not being able to bring up the subject to Mother had been solved happily for her, and she was thankful for that. But what would she expect next?

She had to let Violet know about this. Get her counsel, her wisdom, and her shoulders to cry on. Violet was her closest relative, besides Father and Mother.

But father was no longer around, and mother had been so busy that she didn't seem to care too much about her now. When she spoke to Violet, her cousin as usual was supportive and had some words of advice.

"We have gone through this before, Siu Yoke," Violet said. "Meeting the boy and his family doesn't confirm anything. Just go along and check them out for yourself. At least you get to know what kind of people they are. I don't want to be instrumental in your decision. Whatever it is, you have to decide for yourself."

One week later, over dinner, Mother announced the confirmation of the meeting.

"I met the boy's family last Friday," she said. "They saw the photo of you that I brought with me to the meeting, and they are happy to meet you in person. So we will meet them at their home over dinner this coming Saturday. Go in that lovely blue floral dress of yours."

That Friday night, Siu Yoke had trouble sleeping. She tossed and turned in her bed, her mind filled with so much noise. Every kind of thought rushed through effortlessly as if each train of thought gave way to other trains of thoughts. It was all too noisy for her.

What kind of people were they?

What was this boy like? What were his likes? What were his dislikes? Would she like him?

Would he like her? This was more important, she supposed.

What would her friends at the bank think? Did it really matter what they thought? It was her life. What would Chong Ke think if he found out that she was being introduced to a potential husband again? It was unbearable to even imagine what he would think. No, she couldn't care less, now that they were no longer a couple. Why was she having all these worries? Was she trying to find excuses not to go to the meeting?

It had been almost four years since her relationship with Mr Beh ended. That had been kind of a whirlwind affair, and it had been over almost as quickly as it had started. However, she still bore fond memories of those times with him. He was indeed a kind man, and she felt that he would have made a good, caring husband, and she a good and loving wife. Alas, it was not to be.

Was this going to be a new chapter in her life? She had to be prepared for anything now. She must not forget that her main purpose was to get away from this maddening place she used to call home; a place where she had good memories of Father and all the things that had happened when he was around. Now it was just a place to rest her tired body at the end of the day, in the midst of all the wantonness and sin; the stench of cigarettes and beer and urine each night as she lay in bed.

*   *   *

She woke up Saturday morning with a start. The clock on her bedroom wall read 7.25. She had hardly slept for four hours. Jolted out of her sleep, she felt robbed of a good night's rest. She wanted to just lie there in bed for as long as she could, not having to rush for anything. She had no appointments with anybody that day, except for at the end of the day, so what was the hurry in getting up? She closed her eyes and tried to catch back the sleep she had lost. She could smell coffee brewing in the kitchen. Mother was up and about early. Her eyes still closed, she could hear birds chirping from across the roof somewhere in the neighbourhood. This had some comforting effect on her. As she listened to the chirping and singing of the birds, the trauma of the night soon gave way to comforting relaxation in her spirit. She really didn't feel like getting out of bed. Eyes half opened, she managed to slip back into slumber.

"Siu Yoke. Siu Yoke."

Somebody was calling from outside her door. Siu Yoke turned to the clock on the wall and then jumped out of bed quickly. "Coming."

It was Mother.

"Come have something to eat," Mother said.. "There are plenty of things to do today, and you are still in bed."

"What is there to do, Mother?" Siu Yoke asked..

"You forget we are meeting the Yong family tonight?" This was the first time Mother had mentioned the family's name. "You have to get your dress cleaned and pressed. Your hair needs to be done."

"Yes, Mother. I'll get them done as soon as I can after lunch."

"Good."

When Siu Yoke joined Mother in the kitchen, Mother dished out steaming rice from the pot. The aroma of cooked rice was always so refreshing. It has been a long time that she had a home cooked meal.

Siu Yoke helped with the other dishes. Mother had prepared steamed pomfret, kai lan vegetables, salted vegetable and pork rib soup. All so expertly cooked. Mother had learned to cook at her parent's restaurant when she helped out there many years ago. She had honed her skill since.

Siu Yoke finished her lunch and then helped with the washing up. With a sideward glance, she saw Mother watching her as she did her dishes. As soon as she had finished with that, she went upstairs to her bedroom and took a large white box from her closet. She laid it on the bed, opened it, and took out her pretty blue floral dress. She had worn it for that first meeting with Mr Beh. She was surprised she could still wear it. She was eighteen years old now, and she was pleased that the dress still fit her.

She looked at herself in the mirror and smiled. It still looked new, although it needed pressing. She was relieved that she didn't have to spend additional money for any new dresses.

She took the dress to the living room and ironed it. She didn't want to think about anything now. She was exhausted from all the thinking that she'd done the night before. It was time to relax her mind and think of nothing except how to make herself enjoy tonight. Perhaps the singing birds had helped somehow.

As the time drew nearer to evening, she began to feel nervous. She had not felt like this when she had first met Mr Beh. This wouldn't be any different from that experience, so why was she so nervous? The only reason she could think of was that this time, Father was not around.

There was no turning back now. Mother had been busy buzzing around the house with her usual chores. The new servants she'd hired were not much help. It was not easy getting good help. They tended to laze around when nobody was watching and loved to compare Mother with their previous employers, especially some European families they had worked for who had been generous employers, not only with their salaries but their welfare. Asian employers were not like that.

This time around, Siu Yoke did not want to interfere, since Mother was almost always around these days. She didn't want to fire anyone as she had the other two servants. Besides, her attention was on contemplating if she was making the right decision. She desired very much to get out of this place, and the marriage could be the opportunity for that. So, she would go through with the dinner meeting and hope for the best.

CHAPTER 10

The Meeting

The drive to the Yong family's residence was about forty-five minutes. The Yongs had arranged for a chauffeur to pick them up at 7.00 p.m. They were accompanied by the matchmakers as was customary. It was the fastest forty-five-minute drive Siu Yoke had ever had. It was also the quietest. The matchmakers tried to make small talk, but Siu Yoke paid no attention. She sat in the backseat of the black limousine, staring out at the unfamiliar road they were travelling along. This area was new to her. She had never been to this part of the country. As they drew nearer to the Yongs' residence, the surrounding houses and buildings looked expensive as though only wealthy people lived there.

The driveway to the huge mansion was lined by fig trees. The garden was the size of two football fields, with trees and plants of different varieties. The mansion was four stories high, and the matchmakers said it had been designed and built by the Yong patriarch, and it reflected a European influence.

As the car approached the main entrance to the mansion, servants – both men and women – were there, ready to receive them.

The matchmakers beamed with pride as if they had struck the jackpot. Mother, who had not been to the mansion earlier, also looked excited. It was obvious she had not expected this. She had only met the Yongs at a restaurant the previous week, and she had not mentioned their wealth or where they lived. She had seen a photo of their son, for like Siu Yoke, the son had not been there during the meeting between the elder Yongs and Mother.

Servants opened the car doors and escorted them into the house, all chattering away, their broad smiles making Siu Yoke feel so welcomed. She too was wide-eyed at all she saw. The Yongs' wealth was beyond her imagination. She wondered why a boy from a family like this needed matchmakers.

They entered into a huge hall. In the centre of the hall was a large, round dining table. The Yongs were seated there, waiting for them. The father and mother stood up as Siu Yoke, Mother, and the matchmakers approached the table. The father looked elegant in his European suit, as did the mother in her beautiful green cheongsam, decorated with butterflies and flowers.

The parents beamed with happiness when they saw the young and beautiful Siu Yoke in her blue floral dress, looking so angelic and gentle.

"Oh, you look even prettier in person than you appeared in your photograph," said the mother.

Siu Yoke had no response; she only smiled and nodded.

Their son had also stood when they entered. However, the boy just stood there at the table, not moving. He too was smiling, although shyly. He was pleasantly handsome, with bright laughing eyes and a wide jaw. After all the pleasantries were exchanged, they sat down at their assigned seats. Siu Yoke sat next to the boy, whose name was Long. As she sat, she noticed that he was propped up on a structure that looked like a frame with a seat. He was leaning on this frame and resting his butt on the seat for support. His only movement was from his waist up. It looked like he could not move his legs, which looked slightly bent, although he was wearing long pants and a smart suit himself.

He noticed her sideways glance and bowed head, and he spoke for the first time.

"As you can see, I am handicapped. An operation on my legs went badly, and now I cannot walk."

So this was probably why the parents needed the services of a matchmaker, she thought.

"Long was diagnosed with rheumatoid arthritis," his father said, "which is an autoimmune disease. It resulted in a chronic, systemic inflammatory disorder that affected his joints. We sent him to a hospital for special surgery in New York, but he still came back crippled. We understand if your daughter decides not to marry him, but we can promise you that she will be well taken care of if she does."

Mother was silent. The matchmakers had not told her the truth about the boy's condition when they approached her with the marriage proposal. When she looked at them, they smiled their usual patronising smiles and tried to excuse themselves by saying that they had not known about his condition, which was obviously a lie.

"Our dowry will be a handsome one," continued the father, almost pleading.

They must have had many rejections before, Siu Yoke thought.

"Why don't we enjoy our meal first, before the food gets cold," the boy's mother said quickly. "Come, eat, eat, everybody. Don't

68

stand on ceremony." She picked up a chicken drumstick and placed it on Siu Yoke's bowl. "Come, my dear, this is for you."

"Thank you" Siu Yoke said, trying not to feel sorry for Long.

The rest of the evening was filled with talk about everything except the marriage. It was tense, and Siu Yoke felt it the worst. She was the reason for this dinner meeting.

"Are you working?" Long asked at one point.

"Yes. I work for a bank but I am thinking of quiting." she replied.

"Why? Don't you like the job?"

"No. I like the job."

"Oh. Then why quit?," he said.

The conversation and small talk went on.

Other topics slowly cropped up between them, and their conversation took on a relaxed mood. At times they laughed over silly jokes.

Both elder Yongs and Mother noticed the easy manner between Long and Siu Yoke, and they too became more relaxed in their own conversations.

Unbeknownst to Siu Yoke, the Yongs had made a handsome dowry proposal to Mother, which included taking care of my education costs. It was too good to be turned down, but Mother needed to talk with Siu Yoke about what she wanted. She was pleased to see Siu Yoke was relaxed and comfortable with Long, despite their initial discomfort.

After dinner, the Yongs conducted a tour of their mansion, showing Mother and Siu Yoke around their impressive home with so many rooms. The Yongs had four other sons staying with them in this big mansion, each assigned a room for them and their wives. Their only daughter was married and lived elsewhere with her own family.

The garden surrounding the mansion was huge. Besides the front garden along the long driveway, there was another at the back of the building that was equally large, with a fish pond in the middle. It also had a couple of swings and slides as if in preparation for some grandchildren expected to come along in the near future.

After the tour, it was time to leave. They had been there for over three hours. The Yongs had arranged for their chauffeur to drive Siu Yoke, Mother, and the matchmakers home.

"Bye-bye now," the Yongs said as the party got into the car.

"Hope to hear from you soon," the mother said, waving goodbye.

Long was left on his own, propped up in his chair at the table. Siu Yoke and Mother had already said goodbye to him after coming back from their tour of the property.

As the car moved off along the long driveway, Siu Yoke couldn't help but imagine herself living in a place like this. It would be so very different from Mother's place, the place she used to call home.

What would it be like to be married to Long? Would she really be well treated and taken care of as the boy's father had promised?

"So what do you think, Mrs Pang?" the woman matchmaker asked.

Mother was silent, looking out the window as they drove along Holland Road, back to Serangoon Road. The road was lit on both sides by the dim yellow lights of the street lamps, enough for the driver to see only about ten yards ahead. Shadows of trees and shrubs darkened parts of the road, so he drove slowly and cautiously.

Mother was clearly deep in thought, so the matchmakers left it as that.

Siu Yoke was also lost in her thoughts, watching the bright distant moon follow them. She wondered what Mother was thinking about. She was sure Mother would ask her about the Yongs as soon as they got home. Most importantly, she would want to know if Siu Yoke was prepared to marry the Yongs' son.

It wasn't long before they reached their house on Serangoon Road. The chauffeur came round the car to open the door for Mother and Siu Yoke. The matchmakers also got out there. They would find their own way home, where they would wait to hear from Mother or Siu Yoke.

Mother and Siu Yoke went upstairs to their respective rooms in silence as if each one was waiting for the other to speak up. The tenants were already busy with their business, with the usual cacophony of loud talking and strange men loitering. Cigarette smoke and the smell of liquor permeated the corridor as Siu Yoke walked quickly to her room. This was what she wanted to get away from, she reminded herself. She really wanted to get away from all this. Whenever she went out to meet her friends, they always told her she smelled of cigarette smoke and liquor.

The clock on her bedroom wall read 11.30.

That night, sleep did not come easily. Siu Yoke lay there in bed thinking about the possibility of living in that huge mansion with the Yongs. What would it be like? She would be very far from home. It would almost be like going into Malaya. She had never been to that part of the country before, even when she was with Mr Beh.

Long was good looking too, and he was witty and jovial after their initial uneasiness. How would she answer when Mother asked for her opinion and a decision about the match? The matchmakers definitely would want to know, that was for sure. So would the Yongs.

She felt so burdened suddenly.

Would Mother decide for her, or would Mother allow her to decide, just as Father did in the case with Mr Beh four years before?

The thought of Father brought tears to her eyes again. He had always had her best interests at heart. She hoped that Mother would too, although she would have to abide by Mother's decision if she decided for her.

She had to let Violet know of her meeting with the Yongs. She would be dying to know.

CHAPTER 11

Indecision Is a Nightmare

"He's handicapped!" Siu Yoke said to Violet.

"So what is your decision then?" Violet asked.

"But he seemed like a nice man," Siu Yoke said.

"But what is your decision?" Violet asked again.

"The parents are nice people," continued Siu Yoke.

"Yoke!" Violet exclaimed, jolting Siu Yoke out of her trance-like thoughts.

"I'm sorry," Siu Yoke said, blinking.

"What is your decision?" Violet asked once more, this time impatiently.

"I don't know," Siu Yoke said. "It's too soon. How can I make any decision over just one meeting? Although they seemed to be very nice people."

"So?" Violet asked. "Aunty is definitely going to talk about it."

"I know. But it's been two days and she has not said anything about it," Siu Yoke said. "So I don't know what she is thinking about."

"Why don't you ask her?"

"Why should I ask her?"

"Aren't you interested in finding out?"

Siu Yoke was silent. Maybe she was afraid to find out. Or perhaps she was not ready for any decisions yet, whether by Mother or herself. She needed more time to think it over. It wasn't like playing house. She remembered Violet saying that before.

"Look, Sis, I know it's not easy," Violet said. "I'd hate to be in your position, and I cannot decide for you, but I would encourage you to give this some serious thought."

As usual, Violet was always there to offer whatever advice Siu Yoke needed.

"The ice cream is melting," Siu Yoke said, changing the subject. "We'd better finish them before they turn more watery."

They had met at the Magnolia Milk Bar at Capitol Theatre on this Sunday, to be followed by a movie. It was one of those activities they usually did on weekends when they had nowhere else to go. It was only a bus ride away from home, and the ice cream and movie were affordable.

"I will have to tell Mother that I need some time to think about it," Siu Yoke finally said with conviction.

"Good," Violet said. "Come, the movie is going to start soon. Let's go."

Capitol Theatre usually played imported English films from America. The owner of the Capitol Theatre building was the Shaw family, which had purchased the building from a Persian family, the Namazies, after the Japanese war. They had converted it from a live performance theatre to a cinema.

Siu Yoke could not concentrate on the show at all. Her thoughts kept going back to the Yongs, the dinner, the conversations she'd had with Long, and the tour of their property. She remembered the small jokes they had shared and how comfortable she had become as the night went on. She had enjoyed herself, but she didn't want to tell Violet that. It would be wise to keep that to herself. When she smiled at some of the jokes they had shared, she imagined Violet thought she was enjoying the show. After the movie, as they were walking out of the theatre, she told Violet what she was thinking.

"I think I will want to see the Yongs again, to get to know them better."

"That is what you should do," replied Violet. "But like I said before, don't make any decision without fully understanding what marrying into any family is like."

"That was what Father did when I was matched with Mr Beh. And I think Father would want the same thing in this case too."

"Yes. Uncle has always been a wise man. And we know how much he loved you. He always had your best interests at heart. Uncle would be very pleased to know that you are wise like him."

"Yes," Siu Yoke said, pleased that she finally was clear minded about this. She would speak to Mother about it as soon as she got home.

She and Violet said their goodbyes, Siu Yoke flagging down a trishaw, while Violet went on her own in the other direction.

Upon reaching home, Siu Yoke saw Mother in the kitchen supervising one of the servants in the preparation of dinner. So Siu Yoke went into her room, not wanting to bring the subject up at that time. She had to find a more appropriate time for it, so she decided to wash up and change her clothing.

Dinner was ready at about seven o'clock that evening, which was usual. The tenants never had their meals in the kitchen. They usually ate in their rooms, or they would eat outside the house, in coffee shops or hawker stalls, or at their workplaces.

"Siu Yoke," Mother said in the middle of dinner. "What do you think about the Yongs?"

Siu Yoke was quite pleased that Mother was the one who had brought it up instead of herself.

"They seem to be nice people," she replied

"Not only are they nice people, they are extremely wealthy. You will be well taken care of if you decide to marry their son."

"But he …" A sense of defence came over her as if she were having second thoughts.

"He is not able to walk," Mother said, "but everything else is all right with him. I'm sure they have taken every possible step to make him happy, and you will also be well taken care of."

Was Mother giving her the opportunity to decide, as Father had? Or was Mother working towards forcing a decision on her?

"Can I meet the Yongs again so that we can get to know each other better before any decision is made, Ma?" Siu Yoke asked bravely. This time she felt she would want to exercise some rights; but as soon as she spoke, she almost regretted it, fearing upsetting Mother.

To her surprise, Mother agreed. "That is a good idea," she said.

Siu Yoke was very pleased with herself, as she had made it look like it was Mother who would initiate the next meeting. The matchmakers were equally happy to hear it. It would mean coming closer to closing a deal.

CHAPTER 12

Getting to Know You Better

The chauffeur had picked up Siu Yoke at eleven in the morning to take her to the mansion that weekend for lunch. This second meeting with the Yongs was more comfortable for her. They really seemed to be nice, courteous, and humble people, despite their wealth.

Only Siu Yoke went. She had insisted on it.

Long, as before, was standing at the table with his parents. There was an empty seat on his right reserved for Siu Yoke.

It was a good spread of Shanghainese-influenced food. The Yong patriarch was from Shanghai, having immigrated to Singapore when he was in his late twenties after graduating as an engineer. He had built a very successful construction company over the years.

Throughout lunch, Siu Yoke became more and more comfortable with the Yongs. She sensed their sincerity towards her and noticed their constant attention towards her and Long.

There was plenty of small talk about their favourite foods, activities they enjoyed, and other likes and dislikes. They talked about almost everything and anything, except the marriage, which was what Siu Yoke wanted to avoid too. She was pleased no one mentioned it.

They had desserts after lunch that consisted of cold bean curd and jelly, much to Siu Yoke's delight. That happened to be one of her favourites. So the Yongs had taken the trouble to find out something about her. That was a nice feeling.

After lunch, it was time to relax with some music playing on the radio. A mixture of English tunes and Chinese melodies was played. Then something happened that Siu Yoke was quite perturbed to witness.

Long was tired, having stood there for quite a long time already, and he needed to lie down. Two male servants attended to him. With one on each side of him, they slowly lowered him to a stretcher. The stretcher was on four wheels, and Long used two long poles to move himself around, like paddling a boat.

Siu Yoke was stunned. She had never seen anything like this, but she kept to herself and wondered what else she could expect to find out later.

The elder Yongs excused themselves, leaving Long and Siu Yoke to themselves. As Siu Yoke sat there on the sofa, Long paddled towards her, smiling.

"I guess you were shocked to see that," he said.

She didn't know what to say.

"It's OK," he continued. "I understand. People who don't know me or understand my condition find the whole thing like a circus." He laughed. He sounded so genuine that Siu Yoke laughed along with him.

"But that is not nice, actually," she said.

"Oh, it doesn't bother me much," he said. "I'm quite used to it. But what about you?"

"I think it's a matter of getting used to it," she replied, trying to be diplomatic.

"Listen. I'll understand if you decide not to marry me. You're a pretty girl, and I'm sure you have many suitors."

"No, I don't," she said. "My mother is very strict."

"That's too bad," he said. "It's a waste for you not to have many suitors. Unlike you, I am not, as you can see, an ideal catch for any girl."

"You are talking nonsense, Long," Siu Yoke said. "You are not too bad looking either."

"Look at me, Siu Yoke. Any girl would be mad to want to marry me."

Siu Yoke could not believe her ears. His parents desperately wanted their son to find a marriage partner, and he was talking like that?

"Let's not talk about that now, Long," she said. "Even if things don't work out, I'm sure we can be friends."

"Yes. We can be friends," he said. "But I know my parents will be very disappointed."

"Is this the first time they've used a matchmaker for you?"

"And maybe not the last time," he replied.

"Actually, I was in a match once before, but it didn't work out."

"Didn't work out? Who was the stupid boy who turned you down?" he asked in disbelief.

"We were very happy together, while it lasted," Siu Yoke went on. "But when he found out that I was only fourteen, he felt that I was too young for him. He is quite an old-fashioned person, I suppose."

"I don't understand," he said.

"He was from Taiwan. He was twenty eight years old, and I was only fourteen then. He felt I was too young for him, so we ended the relationship. The matchmakers had not been honest with him about my age. It's the same matchmakers who introduced us."

Long looked perturbed at that.

"It's true." Siu Yoke said quickly.

"It's all right. Don't worry about that. I know it's not your fault," Long said. "Anyway, just like that. he dropped the marriage idea?"

"Yes. Just like that."

"He's crazy," he said. "He must be mad."

Siu Yoke laughed. He laughed along with her, both feeling so relaxed and comfortable with each other's company.

*   *   *

The day soon came to an end, and Siu Yoke had to leave. It was already six o'clock. She had to go home. She felt that she had overstayed her welcome.

"Why don't you stay for dinner?" Long asked.

"I don't think I should," she replied. "I've stayed too long already."

"Nonsense," he said. "It's just another pair of chop sticks."

Just another pair of chop sticks was the Chinese way of saying that it was only an additional person to feed, so it wasn't a big problem. So she accepted his invitation and stayed on.

The elder Yongs were happy that Siu Yoke was staying as they felt that she and Long were getting along very well, even though this was only their second meeting. They were hopeful.

Dinner was another generous spread of roast pork, chicken, herbal soup, and vegetables, all expertly prepared by their cook. It ended with dessert again. This time it was slices of pineapple and papaya.

By then Siu Yoke was feeling tired, and she said that she should be going home.

"Yes. You should go home and have a good rest," said Long's mother.

"We will see you again?" Long asked.

"Yes," Siu Yoke said. "We should get together again."

The ride home was just as long as before, but this time Siu Yoke noticed every tree they breezed by, every shrub, every lamp post, every little bump the car went over. She felt her senses came alive, the same feeling she'd had when she rode in Mr Beh's convertible, feeling the wind on her face and hair. She closed her eyes and enjoyed the ephemeral moment.

Her thoughts drifted back to the lunch, the dinner, and the conversation with Long. He must have been a lonely boy. She hadn't seen anybody else in that big mansion both times she was there, except for the elder Yongs, the servants, and the chauffeur. She wondered where his siblings were.

Mother was anxious to hear about Siu Yoke's meeting. She had been pleased that Siu Yoke had spent a whole day at the Yongs', believing that could mean only one thing, but she needed to hear from her daughter what happened.

"Nothing much, Ma," Siu Yoke said when Mother asked her.

"What do you mean, 'nothing much'?" Mother said. "You spent the whole day with them, and you say there is nothing much? What do you mean?"

"Mother, it was just another get-together, like friends getting to know each other more."

"How can that be?" Mother asked. "You spent the whole day there."

"They insisted that I have dinner with them as well. That's all. Nothing more."

Mother muttered something inaudible as she walked back into her room, leaving Siu Yoke sitting there in the kitchen, deep in thought. Her reverie was abruptly interrupted by the cacophony of noise coming from the tenants' rooms. They all seemed to be shouting to one another. The walls separating their rooms were made of cardboard-thin wood, so they could hear each other well even without shouting, but that had become their standard way of talking when no customers were around.

So, noise now, and then soon, the men would be trudging in with the smell of cigarettes and liquor on their breath.

Enough is enough, Siu Yoke thought.

CHAPTER 13

Violet's Suspicion

"The Yongs are very nice people, Violet," Siu Yoke said, smiling and sipping her pineapple juice after their lunch at Siu Yoke's house. "Of course,." Violet said sarcastically. "I would be nice too, if I wanted something from you."

"What are you saying?" Siu Yoke asked.

"Are you very sure that they are really nice people? Or is it because they want you to marry into their family, and that's why they are so nice to you?"

This remark troubled Siu Yoke greatly, as she had quite accepted the Yong's friendship and had felt their sincerity in her heart. How could Violet cast doubt about them? She hadn't even met them. An ominous wave of doubt flooded through her. She began to feel confused all over again and felt like crying. What if Violet was right?

"Would you like to meet them?" she asked.

"Are you crazy?" Violet asked, her eyes almost popping out of their sockets.

"No. You should come with me the next time and see for yourself what kind of people they are. Then you can tell me how you feel." Siu Yoke was confident Violet would find that they really were nice people.

"I'm not so sure about that, Sis," Violet said. "Doesn't seem right."

"No. It's OK. You are my cousin sister. What's wrong with me going with my cousin sister? You'll be my guest," Siu Yoke said jovially.

"What would Aunty say?" Violet asked. "What would the Yongs say?"

"They will say you are most welcome. Come on. There is no need to think further. You are coming with me the next time."

Siu Yoke reached for the telephone to call Long. After a few rings, he picked up the telephone on the other end.

"Long, I would like my cousin sister to come with me this Saturday. Is it all right?" she asked.

"Not a problem," he said. "She is most welcome. We will arrange for Idris to pick you up at eleven o'clock."

Siu Yoke hung up the receiver and turned to Violet. "See? I told you it's all right," she said. "He said you are most welcome."

Violet still was not sure if this was the right thing to do, and Siu Yoke could see that on her face.

"You don't have to be shy," she said. "They are really nice people."

"We'll see," Violet said.

"So that is settled. This Saturday, you come over by ten in the morning. Their chauffeur will be here at eleven."

"What should I wear?" Violet asked, suddenly panicking. "I have nothing to wear."

"Just dress comfortably," said Siu Yoke. "They are simple people. No need to be extravagant."

"So you are going to meet the Yongs," Mother said. She had heard their conversation.

"Yes, Aunty." Violet looked worried that Mother would be upset with the arrangement. "Siu Yoke wanted me to keep her company."

"I suppose it's all right if the Yongs have no objections. Just go enjoy yourselves."

"Yes, Mother. Mrs Yong said that it is all right."

The dullness that had affected Siu Yoke slipped away, and her feelings were elevated. She felt light, and she was grateful for Violet's presence and support.

Chapter 14

Violet Meets The Yongs

"I have absolutely no idea what I'm doing, coming along with you like this," Violet said as they sat in the backseat of the Yongs' limousine Saturday morning. She didn't understand why she was feeling anxious. It was not her case. It was Siu Yoke's.

Siu Yoke looked at her with a grateful expression; and without her having to say a word, Violet understood that her presence had helped Siu Yoke overcome her own anxiety. She smiled back at Siu Yoke. Now she knew she had a purpose in going, and that was to give Siu Yoke all the support she needed.

Violet was as impressed as Siu Yoke and Mother had been as the limousine approached the main gate to the mansion. The giant fern trees that lined the driveway gave them some shade from the sun, which was glaringly hot that morning. Eyes wide as she stared, Violet "oohed" and "aahed" quietly. Siu Yoke tightened her hold on Violet's hands, silently conveying her appreciation at her presence.

Violet turned to her. "Wow. You should be so lucky."

"You think so?" Siu Yoke asked. "Hey, I've not agreed to the marriage yet, in case you are thinking of that."

"I know. But look at all this," Violet blurted out.

As before, the servants were there to open the car doors for them, and then they escorted them into the house. Violet stood at the doorway, frozen, as she gazed at the wide entrance and the vast hall beyond, with its chandeliers and Chinese scrolls hanging on all corners of the hall.

The elder Yongs came out of their room to welcome them. Violet could feel the warmth of this couple immediately.

"Welcome, Siu Yoke," said Mother Yong, "So nice to see you again."

"This is my cousin, Violet," Siu Yoke said.

"Hello, Aunty," said Violet. "Hello, Uncle."

"Come, come. Come into the living room," said Father Yong. He escorted them towards a sitting area, near where Siu Yoke had dined with them before.

"It's so nice to see you again, Siu Yoke," Mother Yong said as the servants served drinks and snacks.

"Yes, Mrs Yong. It's nice to see you again," Siu Yoke replied. "I hope you don't mind my cousin joining me today." She looked around for Long, which Mother Yong noticed.

"Long will be out shortly," she said "He is in his room changing."

Violet was still amazed at the size of the hall and attempted to look at everything at the same time.

"We will show you around later, after lunch." Father Yong said.

"Hello," Long said as he wheeled himself towards them on his stretcher.

Violet tried hard not to stare, smiling her greeting in politeness as she was introduced to Long. He extended his hand towards her for a handshake, and she hesitated, unsure what she should do.

Long smiled. "Don't worry, I won't bite."

Her anxiety disappeared, and she felt overwhelmed by the young man's pleasant manner, despite his condition. He displayed so much confidence and charm, that same charm that must have won Siu Yoke over. Violet shook his hand and felt his warm grip.

"How do you do?" she said politely.

"I am good, I feel good. How about you?" he replied, beaming a wide smile.

What's with this young man? Violet wondered. Despite his condition, he was bursting with enthusiasm and confidence as she had not seen in anyone else before. She felt Siu Yoke looking at her approvingly and immediately tried to strike up polite conversation.

"Siu Yoke and I are very close friends, besides being cousins," she said. "We go almost everywhere together."

"Then you should come anytime with her," replied Long.

"Thank you," Violet said. "This is such a nice place you have here."

"We'll show you around later, if you want."

"Yes, that would be nice," Violet replied. It was an offer she could not resist.

As they spoke, the servants were busy laying out the cutlery and dishes of food on the dining table, preparing it for lunch. There was a good spread of different types of food: steamed pomfret, roast chicken, sweet and sour soup, and various vegetables, all cooked Shanghainese style again. It was the first time Violet has tasted Shanghainese food, and she liked it.

All throughout lunch, the conversation revolved around how expensive things had become lately and what they usually liked to do during the weekends. A steady breeze coming from the back garden and into the high-ceilinged room kept the air cool. Birds chirping in the back garden beckoned to the crickets to join them in their chorus. It was such a nice and pleasant afternoon that Siu Yoke wished it would last forever.

The calm she felt here, compared to the noisy crowd back home, was such a big difference. She felt an inner peace as she sat there enjoying the company of Long, the elder Yongs, and Violet. Oh, how she wished this would last longer. Then it occurred to her that it was possible. She had to decide if she wanted this badly enough.

Soon lunch was over. Siu Yoke was quite familiar with the estate by then, so she showed Violet around, from the vast hall, to the front and back gardens, from the fish ponds to the garage where a few expensive cars were parked. The chauffeur, Idris, was busy polishing one of the cars. It was the black Cadillac that he had used to pick Siu Yoke and Violet with earlier.

"The Yongs seem to be very nice people," Violet said as they sat on the swing in the back garden.

Siu Yoke was quiet. Were the Yongs genuinely so nice, she wondered, or were they putting on a false front?

"Hey, Sis," Violet said, waking Siu Yoke from her deep thoughts.
"Huh?"

"I said that the Yongs seem to be real nice people," Violet repeated.

"You feel that way about them too?" Siu Yoke asked.

"You don't think so?" Violet said.

Siu Yoke was quiet again. She didn't know how to reply to that. She had her reservations. Should she voice her doubts to Violet?

She should. After all, the whole idea of getting Violet there was to get her opinion about the Yongs.

"Do you think that they are genuinely so nice people, or maybe they're putting on an act?" Siu Yoke said.

"That was what I said the other day. Don't you remember?"

Siu Yoke nodded. "But now that you have met them for yourself, what do you think?"

"Well. If it's a front they are putting up, they will get tired of it.. If they are genuine, time will tell."

"Who doesn't know that?" replied Siu Yoke. "But how much time will that take? I don't want to talk about that now. Let's get back inside, or else we will look very rude to have wandered off on our own on their property."

Returning into the house, Siu Yoke and Violet were greeted by Long, who was now propped up on his tall chair. His left leg was bent slightly, making it shorter than his right leg. He had to wear a platform shoe on his left foot so his stance was balanced.

This time, they all sat on tall bar stools around the tall table, which had been specially made for Long. When they were not expecting visitors, Long would usually have his meals like this, propped up to this table. Now that Siu Yoke and he had become well acquainted with each other, the Yongs felt it was time for her to be exposed to this new aspect of Long's life, to check her reaction and how comfortable she was with it. By now Siu Yoke had grown quite accustomed to it.

"Did you enjoy your tour?" Long asked as they sipped their tea.

"Yes," Violet replied. "You have such a big property. Must take a lot to keep the place up."

"My parents can manage," Long said. "My father is a businessman. He owns a construction company. This house was actually designed and built by him."

This was news to Siu Yoke.

"I guess there are so many things you want to know about us," Long said, looking at her.

She didn't answer. She didn't know what to say.

"It's OK," he continued. "It takes time. There are also many things I want to know about you too."

He was right, of course. They should take more time to find out more about each other before coming to any decisions. But she couldn't help thinking that this place was like a sanctuary, so peaceful and quiet. She could live here forever. She had only been here three times, but she was beginning to feel that she belonged here. Here was the peace and quiet she had been longing for.

Soon, it came time for them to leave. It was nearly five o'clock in the afternoon. The sun had been kind that afternoon, not too hot, allowing plenty of cool breezes to come through. It was like heaven was in their favour. This was something else she felt she missed staying at Mother's house in Serangoon Road. All she could smell the whole day and night there was cigarettes, liquor, and the stench of urine.

The car ride home was filled with girlish chatters and giggling, with Violet teasing Siu Yoke that if she was not careful, Siu Yoke would lose Long to her.

"You can have him, if you want," Siu Yoke retorted. "I won't fight you."

Violet knew she was kidding. They laughed and joked all the way. When they neared Siu Yoke's home, though, the joking and teasing died down. Violet became serious.

"Sis," she began, "do you think you can live a life like that, having a cripple for a husband?"

"He may be handicapped," Siu Yoke said, "but you can see for yourself that he is just as lively as anyone else we know."

"I know. Quite charming too, if I may say so. But don't you find it strange that there was nobody else around? That is a huge house, a mansion, but there are only the three of them, the father, the mother and Long, besides the servants and the chauffeur."

"I understand that most of his siblings are overseas studying, and some of them work. They have their own lives. Maybe we'll meet them the next time."

*   *   *

That night, Siu Yoke once again found sleep long in coming. Her mind was filled with thoughts about the possibility of getting away from this noisy, smelly house to a quiet and peaceful place like the Yongs' mansion. Her imagination went wild the deeper she delved into that train of thoughts. Were the Yongs really such warm and nice people, or was it all an act? Would she be well taken care of if she decided to marry into their family?

As she wrestled with such thoughts, tiredness gradually overcame her, and she fell into one of the most restful sleeps she had ever had.

CHAPTER 15

Unconscious Decision

The usual smell of morning coffee drifted into Siu Yoke's room as she lay in bed pondering the events of the day before. The clock on her wall read 7.15. It was late by her standards, so she quickly got up and headed for the bathroom to wash and change into her day clothes.

Did she want to tell Mother about their visit yesterday with the Yongs, or should she keep it to herself? Would Mother be interested?

Her conversation with Violet had been interesting. Violet seemed to like Long. She had nothing but praise for him. Still, she must not rush into any decision. Who really knew what the Yongs were like? They seemed to be warm and friendly, but that wasn't enough. She had to get to know them better before she jumped into any life-changing decisions. She mustn't be pressured into any decision by anybody, especially Mother.

Mother was nowhere around when Siu Yoke went into the kitchen. Who had been brewing coffee if Mother was not around? Or had Mother gone out after making the coffee, ready for Siu Yoke?

Probably, she thought. She took a cup from the cupboard, poured coffee in it, and helped herself to some biscuits from the biscuit tin.

It tasted good: coffee and biscuits. The air was cool, and she felt an immense peace about her. There was not the usual noise from the tenants, who were a noisy bunch, always chattering like hens in a chicken coop being disturbed by an intruder.

That was strange indeed, she realized. It was not like them. Siu Yoke walked to the stairwell. She could see the downstairs from there; and she also could hear more clearly any conversations inside the rooms, thanks to the thin walls. Nobody was up yet, except for one lone figure sitting downstairs near the veranda, smoking and humming a tune. It was Rose, a singer who had been staying there for the longest time. She couldn't be more than twenty-five years old. Without her makeup, she looked dreadfully tired. Her face was puffy from all the alcohol she drank when entertaining her male patrons.

"Sister Rose," Siu Yoke called from upstairs.

"Ah Yoke," replied Rose. "Good morning."

"Have you seen my mother?"

"She left early this morning for Johor Bahru."

"Any idea when she's coming back?" Siu Yoke asked, although she already knew the answer.

"No. You know your mother. She comes and goes just like that."

Siu Yoke was not surprised at all. It was just like Mother to do that. She would just up and go without so much as a goodbye. At least she had made the coffee for her daughter before she left.

Siu Yoke finished her coffee and stepped back into her room, wondering what she ought to be doing that day, it being a public holiday and she had no plans to go visit the Yongs.

As the morning progressed, she could hear the tenants waking up, one by one, as they called to one another from their rooms. She could hear men's voices also, talking loudly as they walked past her room to the toilet, the familiar odours of cigarettes and alcohol trailing after them.

To her own surprise, Siu Yoke found herself not minding that day. She felt these conditions were only temporary and that she had found an escape from all of this. Somehow, today was different. She could tolerate this house for a short while more, and then she would say good riddance to all that.

She realized she had decided. She would wait to announce her decision when Mother returned.

Chapter 16

Is It So Difficult To Decide

"Are you really very sure about that now?" Violet asked when they met for lunch that afternoon.

"Yes," Siu Yoke said. "The Yongs are nice people, and Long is quite charming. You said so yourself."

"Yes, I know, but I'm not the one thinking about marrying him."

"What are you saying?" Siu Yoke asked.

"I'm not saying anything. I'm just telling you to be very, very sure about this. It's a commitment for life. He's not normal like everybody else."

"Just because he cannot walk does not make him not normal. He's smart, charming, and witty. I think all that are good traits in a person."

'It's your decision, Sis," Violet said. "It's your happiness."

"My happiness?" Siu Yoke said quietly after a while. "Am I happy now? Look at me. Look at the environment I'm living in. Can anywhere else be worse than this? I've lost many of my friends because they feel uneasy about where I live. I don't even dare invite them to my home. Even you feel uneasy whenever you visit me. Don't you?"

This time, it was Violet who was quiet for a short while. She felt empathy for Siu Yoke and understood that Siu Yoke would be much happier anywhere except where she was now.

"I suppose you are right," she finally said. "I wish you happiness with him"

"Thank you, Sis," Siu Yoke said.

"When are you going to tell Aunty?"

"When she returns from Johore Bahru. In the meantime, I will continue to visit the Yongs and Long. You want to come with me?"

"I don't think it's proper," Violet said. "This time you need to have serious talks with them. I don't want to be in the way."

"No. It'll be just another visit, like any other visits."

Violet shook her head. "I think I'll not go this time. You need your private time with them. But don't you think you should tell Aunty first before going to the Yongs with your decision?"

"Of course I'm not going to tell them anything like that," Siu Yoke said. "I haven't decided on it. Anyway, that's for the matchmakers and Mother to do. I'm just going to make my usual visits."

"Yes. You should leave that to them."

"Well, I'll go this Saturday. Sure you don't want to join me?"

"No. I think you'll be all right on your own," Violet said.

"OK. I'll call them later," Siu Yoke said.

As if on cue, the telephone in the hall rang.

"Hello," Siu Yoke said as she picked up the receiver.

"Siu Yoke?" said a voice from the other end.

"Long?"

Violet quickly came next to her as if to listen in, smiling teasingly.

"Stop it," Siu Yoke said.

"What?" Long asked.

"No. Not you, Long," Siu Yoke replied, laughing. "It's Violet. She's making a fool of herself."

"Ah," Long said.

"Nice to hear from you, Long," Siu Yoke said, ignoring Violet.

"I was wondering if you would like to come by this Saturday again," Long said.

Siu Yoke was speechless. What a coincidence. "Yes. That would be nice," she finally replied.

"Lunch?" he asked.

Before she could answer, he continued, "We'll arrange for Idris to pick you at about ten thirty. Is that all right?"

"That's a bit early for lunch, isn't it?" she said.

"Yes, yes. But it's all right, yes?"

"Yes. Of course. I'll be ready by then."

"OK then. We'll see you this Saturday. Bye for now." He hung up.

"Wow. Looks like somebody is in demand," Violet said, continuing her teasing.

"Well, I suppose somebody is jealous." Siu Yoke teased her in return.

"Hey, I have my own boyfriend, in case you've forgotten."

"No, I haven't forgotten. By the way, how is your relationship coming along? Any proposal of marriage yet?"

"Not yet," Violet said glumly. "He has to save up a bit more before that can be brought up."

"I'm sure that won't be too long a wait."

"I hope so too. But I think you will be ahead of me, Sis."

"Left to be seen, Violet," replied Siu Yoke. "Left to be seen."

"What?" Violet asked. "What's there to be seen? You have decided, right?"

"Deciding is one thing. Doing it is another."

Violet looked confused.

"Like you said," Siu Yoke explained, "I still need to find out more about them. What are his siblings like, and so on."

"What does that matter, Ah Yoke? If you are marrying him, what difference does that make about his siblings?"

"Yes, it doesn't make any difference, but at least it's good to know."

"OK. I suppose you're right."

"Sis," Siu Yoke said, "thank you for all your support."

"I'm sure you'll do the same for me," Violet said.

Siu Yoke smiled. Yes, she'd do the same for her.

Chapter 17

Meeting Yun And Maria

Idris came on the dot on Saturday and waited outside the house. From a window, Siu Yoke could see him sitting there in the car, waiting patiently. She took a last glimpse of herself in the mirror before walking out the door. She was dressed in her favourite blue dress, with a white ribbon holding her hair in a ponytail, and white dress shoes. Mother was still not back, so she didn't have to tell anyone she was going out.

"*Selamat pagi,* Nonya," said Idris.

"*Salamat pagi,* Idris," she replied. Her understanding of the Malay language was quite limited, at least she knew how to say good morning.

The sun was brilliantly bright that morning, with scattered, drifting cumulus clouds that offered sheltering shades from time to time. The traffic was not heavy, so the ride to the mansion on Holland Road was smooth and breezy. They reached the mansion in less than one hour.

As always, the servants were on hand upon her arrival, scurrying to open the car door for her with smiles and greetings. She felt so welcomed. She had never been greeted in such a manner in all her life, and it felt good.

Mother Yong and Father Yong were at the huge doorway waiting. Long was nowhere in sight.

"Welcome, my dear" Mother Yong said as she came forward to take Siu Yoke's hand and guide her into the house.

"Good morning, Mrs Yong, Mr Yong." Siu Yoke looked around for Long.

"Long is still in his room," his mother said. "He'll be down soon."

As usual, she was led to the sitting area in the large hall. Servants brought pots of tea and cups as she sat there with the elder Yongs.

"Your dress is very pretty," Mother Yong said. "It makes you look even prettier today."

Father Yong smiled and nodded in agreement, sipping his tea. He was a man of few words.

"Thank you," Siu Yoke said. She blushed and tried to hide that behind her cup of tea. Still, she appreciated the compliment and the warmth in Mother Yong's voice.

The sound of a car coming up the driveway interrupted their conversation.

"That must be Yun," Mother Yong said. "He is Long's elder brother."

So now she got the chance to meet one of Long's brothers.

As Yun walked into the house, he stopped in his tracks when he saw a strange girl with his parents. He hesitated for a moment, wondering if he should move on or walk towards them for an introduction. His father decided for him.

"Yun, come and meet Siu Yoke," Father Yong said.

Siu Yoke politely stood up as Yun approached them.

He was tall with a spring in his steps, and he had the same square chin as Long. His hair was sleekly combed, with a parting in the centre. He looked just as charming as Long and was well built.

"Hello," he said, extending his hand.

Siu Yoke returned the greeting.

"She is Long's friend," Mother Yong said.

"Oh. That's … nice," Yun said with a surprised look. *How on earth did Long get to know such a pretty girl?* he wondered.

There was an uncomfortable silence, until another woman walked into the house. She too stopped in her tracks when she saw Siu Yoke.

"Come," Mother Yong called out to her. "Come and meet Siu Yoke."

"This is my wife, Maria," Yun said as she came towards them.

Maria looked to be in her mid-twenties; and when she took her scarf off, she revealed her curly hair. She was slim and slightly shorter then Yun. She beamed a smile as she approached them.

"Hello, nice to meet you," Siu Yoke said.

"She is Long's friend," Yun said.

"Oh. Nice to meet you, Siu Yoke," Maria said. "That's a very pretty dress."

"Thank you," Siu Yoke replied, blushing again.

Just then Long rolled in on his stretcher.

"I see you have met my brother and his wife," he said as he neared them.

Siu Yoke nodded. She stretched out her hand to give Long a handshake.

He laughed. "No need to be so formal, Siu Yoke. We are friends, remember?"

"Well, we've got to be going," Yun said. "Just came back from the airport and we need to freshen up."

After he and Maria left, Mother Yong said, "They are just married and still young. So they take the time to travel as much as they can, before he settles in to his job with the company."

"Yes," Father Yong said. "My business will one day be taken over by him, since he is the eldest in the family."

Siu Yoke was indeed learning new information with each visit.

"Never mind that," Long said, "Siu Yoke is not interested in all that. Where is Violet?" he continued. "She didn't come with you today?"

"No. She had other things to do today."

"Maybe the next time?" Long said.

Before Siu Yoke could answer, they were interrupted by a servant bringing in a tray with fresh pots of tea and a cup for Long, as well as some cookies on saucers. Mother Yong poured more tea for Siu Yoke.

"Thank you, Mrs Yong," Siu Yoke, letting the aroma of jasmine float to her nose.

"Lunch will be served soon, so don't eat too many of these cookies," Mother Yong said.

"You should stay for dinner as well, Siu Yoke," Father Yong said.

"Pa, we have not eaten lunch yet and you are talking about dinner?" Long said in jest.

"I think maybe not, Mr Yong," Siu Yoke said. "I don't want to trouble you too much."

"No trouble at all," Mother Yong said. "We love your company. There is so much to talk about."

Siu Yoke looked at Long, who gave her a knowing smile. His mother was more interested in her than himself.

Blushing away, Siu Yoke agreed. "If you say so, Mr Yong, Mrs Yong. You are too kind."

"Nonsense, girl," Mother Yong said. "In fact, I do wish that you can come by more often than only once a week."

"Mother, Siu Yoke has other things to do too," Long said.

"Well. I just thought that we … you would enjoy her company."

"Mother, you are embarrassing me now."

"It's OK, Long," Siu Yoke said, feeling very uncomfortable with this conversation. "I can make some adjustments to my schedule and visit you more often."

"Are you sure about that?" Long said. "You come by anytime you want."

"It's all right," she said.. "My mother is often not home. She spends a lot of time going to Johor Bahru for her business."

"What kind of business does she do?" Father Yong asked.

Siu Yoke was caught by this question. What kind of business could she tell him? She certainly couldn't talk about Mother's business at home. What should she say? Then she remembered.

"Oh. She is in some sort of trading. She goes to Johor Bahru to buy clothes and other lady stuff, and she sells them here in Singapore."

"That is good business," Father Yong said, impressed.

Siu Yoke sighed internally, relieved. At least she hadn't lied about that. Thank heavens she had remembered the tenants scrambling to get their hands on the merchandise Mother brought home with her.

The servants were laying out dishes of food on the dining table, and the aromas of steamed fish, roast duck, and salted vegetable soup soon permeated the room. That made Siu Yoke hungry.

Long paddled to his tall table, and two male servants lifted him up and propped him against his chair. It was a sight Siu Yoke had gotten used to by now.

"Come, let's eat," Mother Yong said. She held Siu Yoke's hand and led her to the table.

"How about Yun and Maria?" Siu Yoke asked.

"They will have their own lunch in the other room."

Siu Yoke knew the other room was used when more people were having meals together. It had a round teak wood table that could seat ten people. *That's a very strange arrangement,* she thought.

"Long has four other brothers, including Yun," Mother Yong said. "And an older sister."

"Long is third in line," Father Yong said.

"That is a big family you have, Mr Yong," Siu Yoke said, and he laughed.

"When I first came to Singapore," he said, "I was a penniless immigrant. I had to look for a job so that I could save enough money to bring my wife over from Shanghai. I was fortunate because I met some generous people who helped me along the way.

"I have a degree in engineering, but that didn't help at first. To make a long story short, I learned fast, and soon I was able to start my own small business in property development and construction. It took me many years before I could send my children overseas for their studies."

He looked at Long. "Only Long has not gone because of his condition."

"It's OK," Long said quickly. "I'm happy the way it is. I get pampered."

It was true from what Siu Yoke could see. Both of his parents gave him a great deal of attention. She sensed he was their favourite. Since he had come back disabled from his operation in New York, all he could do was lie on his back or stand propped up in his specially constructed chair. He had told Siu Yoke that when he returned from New York and was wheeled from the airplane on a stretcher, his mother broke down and cried.

Lunch was as usual filled with nice conversations that led nowhere, but at least Siu Yoke got to know more about the family and Long.

She liked him and was beginning to feel sorry for him. Despite his condition, he was jovial and cracked jokes now and then. He seemed to be able to ignore his own condition and focus on other things. He didn't display any self-pity at all and always sounded very positive.

After lunch was over, Yun and Maria appeared from upstairs and joined Long and Siu Yoke.

"Hello again," Yun said. "May we join you?"

"Yes," replied Long.

A servant appeared with a pot of tea and additional cups for Yun and Maria. It looked like they were bursting with questions about Siu Yoke and how Long could have come to know her. Their side glances and almost polite smiles almost made the questions come out, as if they were trying to ask as diplomatically as they could but could not find the right words. So their questions were left unasked.

Polite small talk ensued instead.

"You have a lovely dress," Maria said. "It fits you so nicely."

"Thank you," Siu Yoke replied.

"Your hair is so beautifully done," said Yun.

"Thank you," she said again.

"And those shoes," Maria said. "They go so well with your dress. You must tell me where you got them."

"Oh. They are …" Siu Yoke started to reply but didn't know how to. Mother had brought her dress home from one of her trips to Johor Bahru, and she had picked up the shoes at a shop in the New World Amusement park. They were cheap stuff. She told Maria that.

"Oh, you must show me the shop," said Maria. "They must have lots of other nice shoes, I'm sure."

"Yes. Of course. I'll be happy to show you the shop."

Siu Yoke felt inundated with uneasiness by now. Too much politeness. Too much sweetness. She couldn't take it anymore.

"I think I better be leaving," she said, "I mustn't overstay."

Long seemed surprised. "How about dinner?"

"Another time, Long. I really have to go," said Siu Yoke.

"I'll get Idris to take you." Long said

"Nice to have met you, Mr and Mrs Yong," said Siu Yoke.

"Do come again," Yun said.

Siu Yoke's mind was filled with uneasy thoughts during the ride home. She couldn't understand why she had felt so uncomfortable. They had seemed to be nice people but overly polite. Their sweetness had been overwhelming. She was not used to being in such company.

She wondered if she should apologise to Long for her abrupt departure. Maybe he felt uncomfortable too. He would tell her if he had. She was certain about that.

CHAPTER 18

Confusion and Confession

"Lunch was nice," Siu Yoke told Violet over tea. "And with a great variety of food, as usual."

"And?" Violet asked.

"And what?" Siu Yoke replied, stirring her tea.

"What else? You were there not just for lunch, right? What else? What did you talk about?"

Siu Yoke was hesitant in her reply. She wondered if she should tell Violet about Yun and Maria. Violet seemed to sense her hesitation.

"Long is nice," Siu Yoke began slowly. "His parents are nice, but …"

"Ah ha! There's a *but*," Violet said.

Siu Yoke remained silent.

"But what?" Violet said, almost shouting. "If there is even a slightest doubt, then you can forget about going any further."

"Long is nice. I like him. I also feel that his parents are nice and sincere people."

"You said that before," Violet said. "So what is the problem?"

After a long undecided pause, Siu Yoke said, "I met one of his brothers."

Violet looked at her across the table, waiting, eyes not blinking. "Oh, no. Don't tell me you're interested in his brother?"

"Don't talk nonsense, Sis. His brother has a wife."

"So what's the problem?"

Siu Yoke sighed. "They're, like … I don't know how to describe them."

"Try."

"They were overly polite."

"And that's no good?" Violet asked.

"You don't understand." Siu Yoke tried to explain how she felt, but she couldn't find the right words for her exact feelings "They commented on my dress. They commented on my hair and my shoes."

"They insulted you?"

"No. Like I said, they were so polite. They complimented me on everything I wore, from my hair to my feet."

"And that's no good?"

"I don't know. The compliments came so quickly, I couldn't take it in. It felt unreal. They sounded too nice."

"What's wrong with that?" Violet asked.

"Your hair is nice. Suits you perfectly," Siu Yoke said "Your dress is so beautiful, suits you so nicely. And those shoes. Oh, my, my. They fit you so nicely, as if they were made especially for you. Where did you get them? You really must tell me where you got them."

"What?" Violet said. She stared down at her shoes. "Oh, come on. These old things? You've seen me wear them before …" She stopped as it dawned on her what Siu Yoke was trying to tell her.

"Oh my goodness," she said. "And how did Long take it?"

"I don't know. I didn't stay long enough to find out. I excused myself right after that, said that I needed to go home."

"So what are you going to do now?" Violet asked.

Siu Yoke paused for a while, thinking. "Should I even let something like that interfere with my relationship with Long?" she said pragmatically.

"Hmmm. I guess if you can look the other way, it shouldn't get in your way then."

"Yes. You are right," Siu Yoke said. She was happy with that.

"Well, that's settled then," Violet said, smiling. She was happy for Siu Yoke when she made sense. "So when are you going to see him again?"

"I just had lunch with them yesterday," replied Siu Yoke. "It's too soon to talk about the next meeting, don't you think? But I will probably go visit them next Saturday."

"OK, OK. Just asking. But what about the future?"

"What?" Siu Yoke asked.

"All these lunches and dinners must lead to somewhere, right?"

Siu Yoke stared into her cup of tea as though searching for an answer in the tea leaves.

"You still have doubts?" Violet asked.

What would Father do? Siu Yoke wondered. Father always knew what was best for her. He had been there always, in all circumstances and with all decisions, whether big or small. Her mind drifted back to the time when they had had that first dinner meeting with Mr Beh. Father had said that ultimately the decision was up to her, even if he had found Mr Beh suitable. What would his decision be regarding Long and his family? Would he encourage their match?

Alas, she was on her own now. Mother definitely wanted the match. Otherwise, she would not have agreed to their meeting in the first place. But was Mother more interested in her own benefit than Siu Yoke's? That was something Siu Yoke had to contend with. Mother was more mercenary than Father.

"Are you going to sit there and dream?" Violet asked.

"Oh. Sorry, Sis. Just having some thoughts to myself," Siu Yoke said, having been jolted out of her memory trip.

"You should take the time to think about it carefully."

"Yes, of course," Siu Yoke said.

"Come. Let's go watch a movie," Violet said, changing the subject to ease Siu Yoke's mind. "We can go to Odeon. I think they are playing a Charlie Chaplin movie."

*　　*　　*

The movie was about an hour long. It was a comedy with Charlie Chaplin playing the hero, of course. However, Siu Yoke's attention was not there. Her mind kept drifting off to her meeting with Long and his brother. They all seemed like really nice people, especially the elder Yongs.

What would it really be like if she married Long? What would people think of her marrying into this family? Would they say that she was marrying him for money? That was the furthest from her mind. She enjoyed Long's company. He was always so optimistic and jovial and had never once complained about his condition. She could see that he too enjoyed her company. She had sensed no pretences in him at all during all the times they had been together. He had even said at one time that she must be crazy if she agreed to marry him. That had been genuine.

The movie ended even before she realised it, and the lights came on.

"Well? Did you enjoy the movie?" Violet asked as they walked out of the cinema hall.

"No," was Siu Yoke's honest reply.

Violet was dumbfounded. "What? Which part didn't you like?"

"I wasn't paying any attention to the show," Siu Yoke confessed.

"You still thinking about the Yongs?" Violet asked, exasperated.

"I need some time to myself, Violet. Can we go home now?"

Violet understood Siu Yoke's confused state of mind. Although she was happy to be with Violet, her attention was somewhere else.

"Ok, Sis," Violet said. "But hey, don't think so much. You'll fall ill in no time if you continue like this."

"Don't worry," Siu Yoke said, smiling. "I'll be fine."

Violet was not convinced, but she didn't want to pursue it.

"I have to go home to see if Mother is back," Siu Yoke went on.

Chapter 19

The Decision

Mother was still not home when Siu Yoke got there. Upon entering the house, she met Ah Lan, the youngest of the tenants, around the same age as Siu Yoke, smoking in the hall that led to the kitchen. She was without her usual thick makeup and her hair was tied up into a bun. She looked tired.

"Hello, Sister Lan," Siu Yoke greeted her. "Has Mother come home?"

"Your mother ran away with a man, silly girl," Ah Lan said, sneering at Siu Yoke through the smoke.

"That's not true, Sister Lan," Siu Yoke retorted. "Don't make such jokes. It's not nice."

"OK. Sorry. Just joking. What's the matter with you? You don't look well."

"I'm all right," Siu Yoke said. "Just a little tired."

"Well, you better take a good rest. Do you need any medicine? I have some Chinese herbs that may help boost your energy."

Ah Lan was probably one of the best tenants there. Always minding her own business and staying out of trouble. Not like the others who were so rowdy and loud and always trying to pry into others' business. Ah Lan came from a poor family in Ipoh. Due to her parents' poverty, she had been driven to do what she did. Every month she would go to the post office to send money to her parents. Siu Yoke respected her filial behaviour, despite her occupation.

"Thank you, Sister Lan but I really am all right. Do you have any idea when Mother will be coming home?" Even as she asked, Siu Yoke knew the question was futile.

"You should know your own mother better, Yoke," replied Ah Lan. "She comes and goes without any notice. Today she is here, tomorrow she's gone again. That's your mother."

Siu Yoke knew how true that was, given Mother's propensity to do things without letting anybody know.

"Thank you, Sister Lan. Excuse me now, please. I'll go to my room." Siu Yoke took her leave and left Ah Lan there to finish her cigarette.

Tired and exhausted from the day's activities, Siu Yoke took her bath and went straight to bed, without her dinner. Sleep came easily for her that night.

She was awoken abruptly by some commotion in the hall. There was shouting and screaming and, as usual, the sound of things being thrown. She looked at her clock. It was eleven thirty. She was tempted to go out to see what it was all about but decided against it. What could she do? But the shouting and quarrelling went on for too long, until she could take it no longer. She stepped out of her room and walked towards the commotion.

Two men were yelling at each other; and it looked like they'd get into a fist fight if not for the intervention of some of the ladies, holding them back. Rose was one of them.

"Calm down, Mr Tan," she said. "Do you want the police to come?"

Rose pulled the man aside, but he would not be pacified. He struggled to break free from her hold. Another lady came to help, holding the man back. The other man was brandishing a liquor bottle and swaying from side to side. He was apparently drunk and swearing away, but was also held back by two ladies who struggled under his weight. He was a burly man with tattoos all along his right arm. Siu Yoke thought he looked scary.

Seeing that the ladies had the men under control, she returned to her room, filled with disgust and contempt. She had absolutely no interest in finding out what that was about. All of these goings-on were utterly disgusting. She really needed to get away from this place.

Where was Mother? Why wasn't she around? Mother would be able to stop this fight with no problem. She had seen her mother handle such men before. Mother might appear to be small and genteel, but when she raised her voice, it was authoritative.

The commotion continued. Someone threatened to call the police, but that didn't help. The men were still quarrelling, with the ladies trying to quiet them down.

Siu Yoke slumped into her bed, pulling her pillow over her head, hoping to lessen the din. It helped a little but not enough. It was past midnight now, the time when most of the other tenants would be back from their work. Some would be with men who were just as disturbing and obnoxious. Some of them had regular clients, and these men tended to be more subdued and better behaved. It was the random ones that came back that were rowdy troublemakers. It was as if they knew this would be their only time there, and they could just let off steam and then be gone.

The unending noise and pungent smell were too overwhelming. She would never find peace as long as she was there.

I'll marry Long, she thought. Her decision did not surprise her. He was a nice young man. His parents were equally nice. She didn't want to think about Yun and his wife. As she had said to Violet, she should not allow anything to interfere with her and Long. Yes, that was what she would do. As soon as Mother came home, she would inform her of her decision. Mother would be pleased.

CHAPTER 20

The Final Decision

Two more days passed before Mother finally came home. The trishaw that she came back in was filled with parcels and boxes, and the poor trishaw driver was panting by the time they stopped in front of the house.

After paying the driver, Mother called for Siu Yoke and the others inside the house to come out and help her lug in those parcels and boxes.

"Siu Yoke, your mother is back," Ah Lan shouted as she knocked on Siu Yoke's door.

Siu Yoke was uncertain about how she was going to inform Mother about her decision. Every time she wanted to tell Mother about something, she became ambivalent, and she didn't know why. She hated herself for that, but this time she must be bold. Anyway, she was sure Mother would be agreeable, since she had pursued the match herself.

The boxes and parcels were heavy. They needed two people to carry each one. No wonder the trishaw driver had been exhausted.

The lovely dresses, scarves, handbags, and other trinkets were laid on the long table for all to goggle at. The ladies crowded around, holding up different pieces of the merchandise, comparing how they looked. There was bargaining and hustling all round. Mother was in her element.

Siu Yoke stepped back from all this and observed, admiring how Mother was displaying her business acumen. Mother was sharp. Siu Yoke was not like that, and she wondered why.

She would have to wait till all this settled down before she could get hold of Mother to talk to her. Until then she didn't want to stay any longer. She retreated to her room, finding excuses to tidy up her already tidy room. She looked at the clock. Almost noon. Lunch should be prepared. She usually had her lunch at one o'clock, but she wanted to check with Mother, see if she also needed lunch. She went back outside to the hall, where the haggling was still going on.

She pulled at Mother's sleeve. "Ma, do you want lunch?"

"No, Ah Loi," Mother replied. "I'm busy now."

Siu Yoke went off to the kitchen to start preparing the food. There was kai-lan, bean sprouts, a piece of chicken breast, and salted vegetable soup. She decided to prepare more so that she would not have to cook again for dinner, except to boil the rice. Anxiously, she waited for mother to be done with her business so she could talk to her.

Soon the food was ready. She sat down at the table in the kitchen and set out the dishes of food one by one, being especially careful with the hot soup. All of the food smelled good.

Mother came into the kitchen after Siu Yoke had finished her lunch and was washing the plates. In her hand was a big parcel.

"Ah Loi," Mother said, smiling, "come take a look at this."

She placed the parcel on the table, and Siu Yoke felt it. It was soft. She guessed it was some kind of clothing. When she opened the parcel, her eyes widened. It was a lovely piece of blue silk, soft and smooth to the touch. She brought it up to shoulder height in front of her, admiring its butterfly design. Blue had always been her favourite colour, and she was pleased that Mother remembered.

"It's for you," Mother said.

"Thank you, Ma. You have been away for so long this last time," Siu Yoke went on. "So many things have happened."

"I'm sure everything has been under control," said Mother. "I have been very busy. I did not only go to Johor Bahru. I went further upcountry to Malacca and Kuala Lumpur. There were many things that I needed to purchase, but they were not available in Johor Bahru."

That accounted for the many parcels and boxes Mother had come home with. Previously, when Mother came home, she only brought one or two small boxes.

Siu Yoke didn't know where to begin with what she wanted to tell Mother: her many trips to the Yongs' residence, her meeting with Long's brother and sister-in-law, or the fight that had happened not too long ago.

"Ah Loi," Mother said. "Sit down for a moment. I want to talk to you."

Siu Yoke wondered what Mother had to say. She sounded serious.

"It is time for us to decide on your engagement, don't you think so?" Mother said.

"Yes, Mother. I have been thinking about it."

"But before you say anything, I want you to think carefully about it. You are now eighteen years old. Old enough for marriage. All your cousins are married, and they are younger than you."

"Violet is not," replied Siu Yoke

"Don't talk about her. She has not found anyone suitable yet, or nobody has found her suitable yet."

"That's not true," Siu Yoke said. "She already has a boyfriend. They have been going out for two years."

"Then why are they not married yet? Maybe the boy does not want to marry her? Maybe she doesn't want to marry him? Anyway, let's not talk about them. Let's talk about you."

"Mother, like I said, I have been thinking about it too."

"Whatever decision you have reached, I hope it is the right one."

For a moment, Siu Yoke was silent. What was mother trying to lead her to? She was sure Mother would want her to marry into the Yong family. She paused, almost dramatically, letting the silence to sink in, hopefully giving Mother the impression that she was not in a hurry to get married yet.

"You have been going to the Yongs' residence," Mother said. "You have met with Mr and Mrs Yong's son, Long," Mother said. "What do you think of the family?"

"They are nice people." Siu Yoke remembered how desperately she needed to get away from this house, so she decided to come right to it. "But Long has not asked me yet."

"Oh, not to worry about that," Mother said. "I'm sure he will be more than happy about it. Now, how about you? What is your decision?"

"If Long doesn't mind, then it's all right with me too," Siu Yoke said.

"Good!" Mother said, beaming." I shall let the matchmakers know. Then we will set an auspicious date for the engagement and then the wedding. You will not regret it, Ah Loi," she said as she headed towards the telephone to call the matchmakers about the decision.

Looking at the silk material in her hands, Siu Yoke wondered if she had made the right decision. She must justify it. It had not been an impulsive decision, she said to herself. The marriage would be good for her. She liked Long and felt that love could develop along the way. She had seen many friends get married through matchmaking, and they all ended up loving their spouses. This was especially when the children arrived and completed the marriage.

Would Father be pleased with her decision? Yes, she decided. If he were still around, he would be very happy for her. Most importantly, this would be a good opportunity for her to get out of this house and away from all the shameful goings-on here.

She should let Violet know too. What would Violet say? What would her reaction be? She was her closest relative and she should be informed. That was the proper thing to do.

CHAPTER 21

To Do or Not To Do

"You are very sure about it?" Violet asked when Siu Yoke met her for tea the next day. Violet could not contain her excitement.

"You've met Long. You've met his parents," Siu Yoke said.

"Yes, yes," replied Violet, "but we are not talking about me. We are talking about you. It's your marriage, your future."

"Yes, I know, and I am quite certain about it," Siu Yoke said, though she was reassuring herself more than Violet.

"Well, I am very happy for you," Violet said. "When is the big day?"

"That hasn't been discussed yet," Siu Yoke said. "Mother is arranging it with the matchmakers. I'm sure they will consult the Yongs too."

"Have you told Long?" Violet asked.

"No. What will I say?"

"Well, you should tell him immediately, not wait till later. It's you and him for the future, you know?"

"Yes, yes," Siu Yoke said. "Immediately after this."

"Then, let's go." Violet, hurriedly finished her tea and grabbed her handbag.

"But …" Siu Yoke hesitated, unsure again if her decision was right.

"What now?" Violet exclaimed. "Undecided again?"

I really need to get out of this house. That thought came to Siu Yoke's mind even as she hesitated. With that as her primary reason, she made up her mind. She was not going to have to stay there any longer.

*   *   *

The telephone rang in the Yongs' residence. One of the servants answered it. "Master Long," he called. "It's for you."

Long rolled out of his bedroom to take the telephone from the servant. "Hello, Siu Yoke," he said, his voice ringing with excitement.

"Hello, Long," she said. "Sorry I didn't call you sooner. I have something very important to tell you."

Her voice was trembling and hesitant. After she spoke, there was a longer silence.

Long stayed silent as well, his heart beating a bit faster. His smile slowly dissipated as if wiped off by a handkerchief. He braced himself, remembering the many rejections he'd gotten before, when the girls or their parents announced he was not suitable. He had gotten through those rejections, yet he wasn't sure if he was strong enough to face another one, especially from Siu Yoke. He had not found the other girls favourable. He had felt no love lost in any of them when they rejected him, but this was different. He had found something in Siu Yoke that he didn't see in the others. It would be quite painful if she was going to say no to him too.

"Hello? Are you still there?" Her voice dispersed his thoughts

"Yes," he replied nervously.

"I have to talk to you," she said.

"I'm listening."

"Has my mother spoken to your parents yet?"

"No. Is there a problem? We have not heard from your mother for a long time."

"How about the matchmakers? Have you heard from them?"

"No," Long said. "What is it, Yoke? Don't keep me in suspense. My heart cannot take it." He tried to make it sound like a joke.

"Ha, ha. You are a strong man, Long," Siu Yoke said. "But I want to tell you in person. Not like this, over the telephone."

"Oh, no," he said. "Good news or bad?"

She was silent. The short moment felt like eternity to Long.

"You will know when we meet," she said. "Can I come to your place today?"

"It's that urgent? OK, I'll get Idris to pick you." Long was getting more concerned. What was she going to say to him? He had to brace himself.

After he hung up, he called for his parents.

"Ma, Pa, have the matchmakers or Siu Yoke's mother spoken to you yet?"

His mother looked at him worriedly. She had not seen him like this before. He looked nervous and anxious over something.

"No, Long," she replied. "I guess they have not come to any decision yet. Is there a problem?"

"Siu Yoke said she has something important to talk to me about, and she is on her way here now."

"Any idea what it is about?" his father asked.

"I don't know what she wants to talk about. She sounded upset, and she has not sounded like that before when we've spoken on the telephone. She said it is important and that she will only talk to me in person, not over the telephone."

Long sounded despondent, almost downtrodden.

"Oh, don't think so much," his mother said. "You don't know what she is going to tell you." She felt sorry for the young lad. She knew as well as his father that Long had suffered numerous rejections before, and they knew how badly he felt each time. In fact, they did not know he hadn't been that hurt by those previous rejections, or that he was truly attracted to Siu Yoke. She seemed the right one for him. If only she felt the same.

The long wait for Siu Yoke's arrival was torturous.

Lunch was served, but Long did not feel like eating. His mother urged him to eat something, even if not much. He agreed, but most of the time he was playing with his food, something which he had never done before. His mother could see that he was truly not himself. Conversation over lunch was minimal. Often, the only sound was the utensils clanking on the plates and bowls of rice and food.

Then the telephone rang again, startling them out of their uneasy quietness.

*   *   *

Siu Yoke recognised the black Cadillac as Idris rolled to a stop in front of the house. She had just finished tying her ponytail as she came down the stairs to the door. She was having mixed feelings about what she was going to do. Was it right for her to go to inform Long about her decision personally? Since Mother had not informed the matchmakers or the Yongs yet, she should take the opportunity to do it. As Violet had said, it was their future and nobody else's.

125

At the back of her mind, though, she felt a nagging uneasiness that it was not proper to bypass Mother or the matchmakers. How would they feel if they found out she had announced it unofficially? It was not customary for any person that was being matched to do so.

This indecision kept creeping into her mind as she sat there in the back of the Cadillac as it rolled along Serangoon Road towards Holland Road. The road was surprisingly clear of traffic, so the trip was quite pleasant without much stop and go. But Siu Yoke was too preoccupied to appreciate the smooth ride.

As they approached Dhoby Ghout near the Cathay Cinema, Siu Yoke called out to Idris.

"Encik Idris, can you turn back around and go to my house? I've changed my mind about going to the Yongs' house."

Idris was caught by surprise by this sudden instruction. Siu Yoke usually kept to herself and had never spoke during all their previous rides.

"But, missy, Towkay Long is waiting for you," replied Idris, looking in the rear-view mirror.

"It's all right, Idris. I will telephone him immediately when I reach home."

Idris didn't know if he should take her instruction or stick to the Yongs'. "Missy, I will get into trouble if I take you home instead of to Towkay's house."

"Don't worry, Encik Idris. I will explain to them. Please, Idris. I cannot go there today. It's important that I don't go today."

He saw the desperation in her face, heard the urgency in her voice.

He reluctantly made a turn onto Stamford Road and headed back to Serangoon Road.

"Thank you, Encik Idris," Siu Yoke said with relief.

*   *   *

Siu Yoke reached for the telephone and dialled the Yongs' number. It rang for a while before one of the servants answered. She felt her heart beat faster, her hands perspiring as she waited for Long to come to the telephone.

CHAPTER 22

The Telephone Call

Long picked up the telephone and was surprised, even concerned, when he heard Siu Yoke's voice. "What happened? Have you not left home yet? It's been over an hour since Idris left to pick you."

"Long, I'm afraid I changed my mind. I'm not coming today," she said apologetically. "I'm sorry."

"Why? What's the matter?" he asked, getting more anxious. "You said you have something to tell me personally. So what is it?"

"I think I'll leave that to my mother and the matchmakers to inform you and your parents, Long."

"Why can't you tell me? Is it serious?"

"It's better I leave it to them to tell you. Please understand. It's not proper for me to say."

"You are making me very anxious, Siu Yoke," Long said. "Can't you just give me a little hint?"

She kept silent for a long while, which made he made him more upset.

"I think you'll be hearing from them very soon, so just be patient," she finally said.

"Is it good or bad?" he persisted.

"Let them tell you."

"What kind of an answer is that? Stop playing games, Siu Yoke." He was now getting agitated. It was not his nature to be so, but he could not control himself.

"Long. Please just be patient. You'll hear from them soon."

Long kept quiet for the longest time. "I suppose you have your reason," he finally said, "and I respect that."

"Thank you. I have to go now. Bye."

With that, she hung up, leaving Long staring at the telephone.

"What is it, Long?" his father asked as Long paddled back to where they were sitting.

"That was Siu Yoke," he said. "She is not coming."

"What about what she had to tell you?" his mother asked.

"Her mother or the matchmakers will call us."

"What is their decision, then?" his mother asked, concerned about his feelings.

"Don't know," he replied. "She didn't want to say."

His parents were silent. Now they were also getting anxious over what decision Siu Yoke and her mother had made. Primarily, they were concerned about how any negative decision would affect their son.

Chapter 23

No Turning Back

Siu Yoke waited for Mother to come home that night. She could not wait till tomorrow, since she had made up her mind and was afraid that she might change it if she waited too long. She wondered again what Father would do in this case. Would he be supportive of her decision? But he was no longer around for her, and she had to make her own decision.

The stench of urine drifted into her room again, carried by a small breeze.

That broke her thoughts, and immediately, past events in that house intruded into her mind: the endless parade of drunken men, smoking and shouting vulgarities; the quarrel she'd had with the servants; the men that came barging into her room; the tenants' constant yelling. All these became the catalyst for her to decide to get out of that place. Marrying Long was a good escape route. She only hoped she was not jumping out of the frying pan and into the fire.

In the midst of all her mental wonderings, she fell asleep, unable to control her tired body. She drifted into a restless sleep, broken once in a while as her ears strained to hear if Mother had come home. The noise of the tenants and their men visitors also disturbed her sleep. She wondered if she should leave her bedroom to look for Mother, in case she had actually come home, but then she decided against it. She didn't want to have an encounter with any of the men. So she lay there in her bed, waiting, drifting in and out of sleep.

It was about twelve thirty when she heard someone calling her name. It was Mother. Siu Yoke jumped out of bed sleepily, but she was happy and relieved.

"Ma," she said to Mother.

"Ah Loi," Mother said, entering the room.

"Ma, I have something to tell you," Siu Yoke started, but Mother interrupted her.

"I was at the Yongs' residence with the matchmakers," Mother said. She looked at Siu Yoke as if waiting to see her reaction to what she had just said.

Siu Yoke, though, just sat on her bed and waited for Mother to continue. Since she said nothing, Mother continued.

"I think you are comfortable with the Yongs, and especially Long?" Mother said.

Siu Yoke nodded, waiting to hear what more Mother had to say.

"In that case, I just want to confirm with you that you have no objection to the marriage?"

"Yes, Mother. I am all right with it.. What did the Yongs say?"

"Of course they are happy with it. They are just waiting for our decision. Since you feel comfortable with them and Long, we will go ahead and make the necessary arrangements. We will select an auspicious date and time and make the announcement to all our relatives and friends."

"Yes, Mother," Siu Yoke said, her voice almost inaudible.

Mother looked surprised at Siu Yoke's ready agreement. "All right then," she said. "Tomorrow I will talk to the matchmakers and announce it to the Yongs. You go back to sleep now."

With that, Mother walked out of the room, leaving Siu Yoke with her thoughts. There was no turning back now. She has agreed to the marriage, finally. She was sure that Violet would come to know it soon.

CHAPTER 24

The Final Goodbye

Siu Yoke telephoned Long the following Friday. When he came on the phone, his voice was all peppy and cheery.

"Your mother and the matchmakers came by two days ago and said that the marriage is on. You have decided on that?" he said.

"Yes. It was a mutual decision actually, Mother and myself."

"You are very sure about it?" Long asked. "The marriage, I mean."

"Why?" Siu Yoke asked, surprised.

"I mean, I'm not like other men. I'm –"

Before he could finish his sentence, Siu Yoke interrupted him.

"What? Are you mentally unstable? Or are you a monster? Or do you have some terrible disease?"

"No ..."

"So what's the problem?" Siu Yoke asked.

"You're mad," Long said. "But I'm happy about it."

"So am I," she said. She could feel his smile over the telephone.

"So, will you be coming over this weekend?" he asked.

"No. I don't think so. There are many things to be done, and Mother wants me around more to help out."

"All right. I think we also have a lot of things to do, although I will not be helping out much. My parents will get things organised."

*   *   *

The following week was a flurry of activities. Mother made enquiries with several restaurants for the wedding dinner. It would not be too extravagant, as she would only invite close friends and relatives. She consulted for an auspicious day from fortune tellers who knew something about feng shui for the date of the dinner. Mother and the Yongs also consulted about the auspicious day for the wedding, which was set for three months from then. After finalising the date, wedding invitation would be sent out and special ornaments would be bought. Special auspicious food would be prepared for the morning of the wedding, to be eaten before the bride left her mother's home for her future home. Then there was the wedding gown and shoes that Siu Yoke would be needing.

Violet dropped in more often than before to give a helping hand. She was just as excited as Siu Yoke and bubbling all over with joy. She also went along to help choose the wedding gown and shoes for Siu Yoke, and both girls giggled and teased each other just as much as before.

"So when will your day come, Violet?" Siu Yoke asked.

"Ah. He has to save enough before we can talk about it." Violet paused and then grinned again. "But it shouldn't be too long now."

"Oh. So we are getting somewhere now, huh?" It was Siu Yoke's turn to tease her.

"Yes. We have talked about it. Our plan is next year."

"I'm so happy for you. And don't you dare forget to let me help out when the time comes. You understand?"

"Yes, yes," Violet said. "I wouldn't dare not to."

Both girls went on sharing their ideals and ideas about what they would expect out of their marriages, sometimes exaggerating for the fun of it.

Mother had listed the names of all the relatives and friends she would invite. Siu Yoke also had some friends that she wanted to invite. She considered Chong Ke. Should she include him in her guest list? She decided not to. After all, they had not been in touch since she went out with Mr Beh, and she did not know how to reach him. But she would invite her friends from the bank. They would be happy for her too. She also needed to tender her resignation from the bank.

It was not a very long list. The number of invited relatives and close friends of Mother's came to thirty. Siu Yoke's list was no more than fifteen.

*   *   *

The announcement was made. Three months of preparation. All the relatives and friends were notified. Well-wishes came quickly. There were trays of different types of food that were only prepared before a wedding. The tenants were excited for Siu Yoke, and many had gotten her gifts, much to her surprise. She decided it was because of the atmosphere of an impending wedding. Most of the tenants had never been married, or were separated from their spouses. Many of them were from the Malaya mainland and had left their families in search of better lives here. They were hopelessly dismayed when they couldn't find any and had to resort to doing what they had to do in order to be able to send money home to their families.

The Yongs had sent gifts too, among which was a roast suckling pig, a symbol of the bride's purity, which meant she had not been touched by another man. This gift was customary. They also gave two red envelopes containing money to Mother as a token and dowry for the hand of Siu Yoke in marriage, and to Siu Yoke. It was not a small amount. Mother kept all the money, while Siu Yoke got to keep the gifts that suited her: dresses, makeup, perfume, and many other girlish things. She and Violet were impressed at all the expensive brands, the sort which neither of them could afford to buy on their own.

As the day of the wedding drew nearer, one Sunday afternoon over tea, Violet said,

"Well, Sis. Finally, huh? No regrets, I hope."

"Don't talk rubbish, Sis," Siu Yoke chided, "What is there to regret?"

"I'm sure the Yongs will treat you very well," Violet said. Siu Yoke fell silent, and Violet noticed a sudden change in mood.

"It's too late now, Sis, if you're thinking about changing your mind," Violet said.

Siu Yoke looked up at her, eyes gleaming with glee. She was overwhelmed with joy but couldn't find the right words to express herself.

"I shall pretend I didn't hear you say that." She laughed. "I couldn't be happier, Violet," she continued. "I'm getting married. To someone that I happen to like too. Change my mind? Of course not."

"Only like?" said Violet. "What about love?"

"Love is for the Western people," Siu Yoke replied philosophically. "It's more important that love be developed in a marriage. That is much better than falling in love and getting married, only to fall out of love. Don't you think so?"

Violet looked at her with admiration. "Wow. That is so true. If that is the case, what about me and Loke?"

"Don't let me spoil it for you," Siu Yoke said. "Your case and my case are different. We think differently. We were brought up differently. That was what Father taught me, and I believe he was right. He and Mother were like that, and they had a very happy marriage."

"I couldn't agree with you more," Violet said. "I believe you will be very happy with Long."

*   *   *

A month later, a week before the actual wedding, Siu Yoke's dinner was held at the Chinese restaurant at the New World Amusement Park. A wedding dinner was customary, so that all the relatives and friends could share the happiness of the bride to be. It was a happy moment for Siu Yoke. The Yongs were not at the dinner. They were arranging another one on another day. Siu Yoke and Mother would be there, of course, along with some of their closest relatives.

She wondered what it would be like if it were with Mr Beh. Perhaps the wedding dinner would be different. She wondered if Father would be happy for her too. She wondered if Father was watching over her. She missed him. Her eyes welled up again when she thought of him. She was sure that he would be happy for her.

*   *   *

One week later, the Yongs held their wedding banquet at their enormous mansion. Hundreds of guests attended and extended their well-wishes and gifts to the Yongs and Long. The banquet was much more elaborate than Siu Yoke's. There were more than twenty tables, filling the large garden and the main hall of the mansion. A band was also engaged to liven up the dinner.

*   *   *

The day finally arrived. Siu Yoke was awake at dawn, full of excitement and anticipation. Her white wedding gown hung on the rack in her room. Mother was already up and making all the preparation to let go of her daughter. She called Siu Yoke to her, and together they paid respect to their ancestors, burning incense and setting offerings of fruits and food on the altar. Father's photo was there, and he was smiling as if giving his blessings. Siu Yoke looked long at his handsome face, smiled, and said her goodbye.

Violet was there. She had slept over with Siu Yoke, chatting away the night, reminding Siu Yoke of things they used to do. Now that one of them was getting married, they might not be doing so much of their girlie things. Other relatives were there too to celebrate the happy day.

Uncle Tim was there. He was a stout, well-muscled man who worked at a rice warehouse along the Singapore River, carrying sacks of rice from the boat to shore. Daily work like that had helped build his strong stature. Other relatives, uncles and aunts Siu Yoke hardly ever saw, were there too, along with some neighbours. All had gathered to congratulate her and wish her a happy future.

The special bridal food was there, spread over the long dining table for everyone to enjoy. The tenants were, surprisingly, very well behaved. Not one of them let a foul word come out of her mouth. Siu Yoke and mother were very pleased with their change of behaviour, although they suspected it was only temporary.

At 11.15 a.m., an entourage of four cars drove up to the front of the house, all expensive American brands, all decked with ribbons and white flowers. Siu Yoke recognised the first one. It was the one that Idris always used to pick her up with. Idris was driving, as usual.

The Yongs had sent Long's closest friends and relatives to "invite" the bride. Eleven fifteen had been declared the auspicious hour when the bride had to leave her old home for her journey to her new home.

Some of her belongings had already been sent to her new home a week earlier, so she did not have anything to bring with her.

It was a sight the neighbourhood had never seen before, and everyone was there cheering for Siu Yoke. It was such a grand affair and would be the talk of the neighbourhood for the next few months.

Amidst firecrackers and the banging of gongs, Siu Yoke – dressed in her wedding gown – and Mother walked to the black Cadillac that Idris was driving. Siu Yoke turned around to give the neighbourhood one last look and then slipped into the car with Mother. As the entourage drove off, she gave one more look to the house where she had such fond memories of Father.

THE END

Printed in the United States
By Bookmasters